PLAYING WITH FIRE

DAVID TIENTER

PLAYING WITH FIRE

By

David Tienter

Published by Enigma Press

(An Imprint of GMTA Publishing)

GMTA Publishing
6296 Philippi Church Rd.
Raeford, NC 28376

Printed in the U.S.A.

ISBN-13: 978-0692262047
ISBN-10: 0692262040

DEDICATION

I want to thank my two lovely daughters, Jennifer and Anna. Their faith in me and their encouragement was so helpful.

TABLE OF CONTENTS

Chapter One 5
Chapter Two 9
Chapter Three 21
Chapter Four 24
Chapter Five 30
Chapter Six 39
Chapter Seven 41
Chapter Eight 46
Chapter Nine 56
Chapter Ten 60
Chapter Eleven 64
Chapter Twelve 68
Chapter Thirteen 70
Chapter Fourteen 80
Chapter Fifteen 88
Chapter Sixteen 90
Chapter Seventeen 94
Chapter Eighteen 97
Chapter Nineteen 98
Chapter Twenty 103
Chapter Twenty-One 109
Chapter Twenty-Two 112
Chapter Twenty-Three 123
About the Author 130

CHAPTER ONE

MATT 1967

Day starts early. Black everywhere, I rise from the cot, throw on my flak jacket, grab equipment, weapons, and move at double time to the Huey, joining with my team as I go. Zsabo is already there. Intel has been radioed in. A VC heavy has been located. We are being sent to snatch him, should return by noon. We carry no food, one canteen. The throb of the rotor is soothing and I quickly nod off. As always, I sit on my helmet. Too many bullet holes in the Huey to think aluminum walls can protect you. I carry an A-40 Sniper Rifle, a 45 cal. pistol in a hip holster and a 38 cal. pistol in an ankle holster. I sling my medical bag over my right shoulder.

I am a Navy Corpsman attached to the Marines. I love the Navy, but the Corps is my home. I have been lucky to be accepted into this elite group, Force Recon. More than two years of advanced training has been needed for me to be going on this mission. I may be going into hell, but it's with my brothers who can handle hell. I am not worried. Whatever happens, I can think of no greater honor than to be here with these men.

Forward movement stops, ropes go out the door, Lieutenant Zsabo checks the first man's rappelling gear. Less than a minute later, we are grouped on the ground, moving toward our objective. No talking now, only hand signals. Our eyes have adjusted to the dark but we still need to be close to see his hands.

By the time dawn begins to break, we are in position. I am twenty feet up a pine tree on the edge of the village where I can easily cover everyone with the rifle. They begin the search with the first hooch on the edge of the village. Sgt. Meese brings out six natives. They are passive, immediately go into the Vietnamese squat.

Then the first shot rings out. I see cone-hatted heads popping up everywhere. The Marines form a circle fighting outward, I drop the first five enemy that I can get into my sights, scramble down the tree, and run towards the Marines. I feel more than hear an explosion to my left. I am thrown to the ground on my right side with my left knee locked up to my chest. When I looked at it, my knee cap has been forced to the left side of my knee. I gripped it and force it back into place on the top of my knee as I straighten my leg out. White lights of pain guide me into the deep black of unconsciousness.

I wake up tied up by my wrists to a long bamboo pole. My left knee looks the size of a volleyball and I'm bleeding from at least five small holes on the left side of my body. Easy to see them, I am wearing no clothes. I have no shoes either. The harsh smell of gunpowder fills my nose. The residue from the blast coats the right side of my body. There are four other Americans tied to the same pole with me. I don't know any of them. No idea what has happened to my team. Clearly I am a prisoner, I assume the worse, pray for the best.

We are The Show. VC propaganda on a bamboo stick. They lead us into a village and call everyone out. The elders just look at us, the kids poke at us and kick our legs. The younger people throw dirt water and call us G.I.'s. Don't want to know what's in the water, but it smells like urine, I expect my wounds will be infected. We are marched through two more villages.

At twilight, we are given a half cup of rice and still tied to the bamboo, forced to sit on the river bank. The bamboo is secured between two large boulders. By stretching against the pole, we can just get our mouths to the river's edge so the water we can get is half mud. Their leader, 'Uncle Ho,' comes by to tuck us in with a gentle boot to the head. Before nightfall the other prisoners are asleep. I sit up and begin to chew at the wire binding my wrists.

It's an awkward position, painful for my teeth, but if we do not escape, we are doomed. The insects will insure our death if the exposure, infections, and starvation do not kill us first. I chew and try to break the wire. I bend my wrists and arms, move the wire with my teeth and gradually I begin to feel it weaken. I have lost one of my incisors already, but I continue. I can always gum my food. First stay alive. Finally, I feel it break. I work one end around the pole with my mouth. I hurry knowing that if I am caught they will kill me. My mouth is bleeding freely now. The blood helps lube the wire and I slip one hand out and unwrap the other hand. I hold one hand over the mouth of the man next to me and awaken him. “Silence is life.” I untie him. Much faster with hands. He is very quiet and repeats what I have done for him to the next man. When both men are freed and untying the men next to them, I slip into the stream and quietly let the current take me down stream. I dog paddle to the deeper channel and feel the current begin to pull me along quicker. Suddenly a sneeze, wild splashing then gunfire on the shore. Can't see what is happening, can't help anyone there. My heart wishes them the best. Hope some make it. A large branch floats past me and I pull myself up onto it. When I see light beginning to break in the east, I swim to shore and enter the jungle. Traveling on the river is easier, but I don’t know where it’s going or who is along its banks. I'm lost, naked, unarmed, and hungry. Not a good prospect for survival in enemy country. At least I am hydrated.

I crawl into the jungle a few yards and stop. I need to think. If I hurry now, I die. If I panic, I die. I have only one weapon, my brain, I have to use it to survive. I stand and begin walking slow, I watch. Soon I find large leaves and wrap my feet, held on by vines. Snakes are the easiest food to find and kill. Hoping they don't find and kill me first. I learn, I watch everything. It is safe to move when the animals and birds are quiet. If I move very slowly, they don't react. If they are nervous, someone or something is around. This is the land of water buffalo's and tigers. Buffs hate us and want to trample us, tigers love us and want to eat us. On the fourth day, I kill an enemy soldier. I know within ten seconds of seeing him that he is alone. I can smell the fear on him. I watch him moving down the trail. Short steps, not confident strides. His rifle is at the ready, he is wary, too hesitant, an undercurrent of fear. A man leading a company walks easy. Assured by the safety of numbers.

Once he passes where I am hidden, I step out, grip his head from behind and break his neck. Now I have a rifle with 12 rounds, a knife, pants to wear – held up with vines. The pants are much too small, but they protect tender areas. I find the picture of a smiling Vietnamese cutie. The picture looks the same as many others I have seen and I wonder if they are all given the one picture and a promise of happiness with her after the war. His rations, such as they are help for two days. His shoes are sandals made for children, much too small, and his jacket has VC insignia. Death if I am caught wearing it. The biggie is the knife. Life is much easier with a knife. I use the sun for directions, move slowly, spend a lot of time worrying about tigers, and find raw cobra is the best tasting snake meat.

Three months later, I step out on to highway 1 near Da Nang, in front of an armored patrol. They are not sure what to make of me, but the Marine Corps remembers me. Hot food, medical exam, new clothes, and they call my folks to let them know I am still here among the living.

The best part for me is the letter from my wife, who complains to me that her marriage to Ray had to be annulled and she is being forced to repay the life insurance and she will lose the Porsche she purchased with it. My actions have never made her happy anyway. It's the little things that make life good.

CHAPTER TWO
PRESENT DAY MATT

I have a salmon hooked and running. He took my Shiny Angel on the third cast of the morning. A big fish, for a fly rod at least ten pounds of flash in the early morning light. There is only a six pound tippet attached to the fly. Gently, I must treat him very gently. On his first run he takes out over 120 yards of line, in an upstream run, before I can turn him. His speed is incredible. Unable to reel in line fast enough to keep the line taunt as he rushes back at me, I fear the slack line will allow him to spit out the fly. It's exciting to find him still on the line. He's running down stream this time. He leaps and the morning sun sends him into a prism of colors. Trying to keep him off the bottom so the line won't snag on any obstruction, I walk downstream as rapidly as the old pegs can move, trying to keep up. Stumbling in the wet sand and almost falling, I recover my balance and manage to turn him. He must be tiring. Dipping my hand net into the water so that his scales won't be damaged, I bring him close enough to land. He is spectacular. I net him, drop my pole, and use my forceps to remove the fly from his lip. I gently return him to the water. He is too valiant to be harvested. He will live to fight again. I can have a fried egg sandwich for breakfast.

Many of my friends use a gym to stay in shape. They play cards and brain games to keep alert. I have fly fishing. The hike out to the fish, the actual physical action needed to cast a fly and retrieve a fish works for me physically. The necessary assessment of water conditions and recognizing which hatch is under way so I can use the appropriate fly helps to slow the mental deterioration.

I am camped at Cedar Creek, near the Ouileute Indian Reservation in Olympus National Wildlife Park, in northwestern Washington State. The beauty of the area is a delight to my senses every day. Mount Olympus to the east and the ocean to the west, make this a remarkable place.

After being here for six weeks, I can feel that it's time to leave.

The cold weather is forcing me to seek warmer climes. The mornings have taken a significant dip from crisp, which I like, to cold, which I find unpleasant. It's difficult to get my toes warm, lately. I find my tent adequate up to this point especially with the abundance of beauty all around me, but I can see snow moving down the sides of the mountain. I know I will return again but it will be during the summer. In my younger days, I would have stayed the winter. Now, approaching seventy, with a prosthesis in my left knee, taking an oral chemo dose from a previous cancer operation, and the progressive diseases of age, my body becomes too stiff and painful in the cold wind. It's becoming harder to motor this two hundred and twenty pounds around. A widower now, I lost my life's love almost a year ago. I still catch myself waiting every morning to hear her voice telling me to, ' hurry, dear, the coffee is ready.'

Now I travel and camp, living the life I missed while earning a living. I loved camping as youngster. My father introduced me to the wonders of nature on weekend overnights in the beautiful bluff country of Southeastern Minnesota. The small spring-fed creeks were alive with brown and rainbow trout.

Back then, it was sit on the ground, old woolen army blankets for tents and sleeping bags, and a thin supple sapling with a line tied to it for a fishing pole. We always ate hot dogs, cooked at the far end of a thin branch, and pork with beans, eaten straight from the can. The sky was brilliant at night with the Milky Way and shooting stars putting our small town Fourth of July fireworks to shame. These were the best times I ever shared with my father. He was a gruff man, sadly, feeding and housing his family absorbed most of his energies. These few weekends were the best times and memories I have of him.

Coffee is brewed, nice fire is encouraging me to cook breakfast. I am starting to relax when I see a man moving up the beach toward me. He is still too far away to identify, but he walks with that stiff upright stride of a cop. He is obviously looking for me as there is no one else camped near me this morning and he is clearly not dressed for the beach. He's wearing new jeans, new shirt, new sneakers, and covers it all with a green police jacket. A camo cap completes the ensemble. No fishing pole. As he gets closer, I recognize him. It's Frank Johnson, a friend from South Dakota. I feel my neck tingle, bad news is coming, he didn't come fifteen hundred miles for a casual chat. At least, the government issue jacket he's wearing will keep him warm so he won't have to hurry to get out of the cold. Frank has always been one of the good guys, a Deputy Sheriff, for a small farming county in South Dakota. We had worked together to catch and punish his wife's killer.

I had been staying at his house visiting, when tragedy struck. While Frank and I were out, his wife was brutally murdered. Working together, we uncovered her killer. The killer turned out to be a woman who sang in the church choir with Jenny. Frank and I traced her movements across three states and then completely ignoring the law, we made sure she paid for her crime. She will never get out on parole. Dirt naps have no parole.

"Hi Frank," I shout at him while he is still half a block away.

"Hey Hey, Matt, you old fart, imagine meeting you out here," he says. "You got any coffee left?"

"What the hell kind of question is that. You never saw the time I wouldn't have coffee. Help yourself. I am making sandwiches, want one?"

"No thanks, stomach is a little queasy from the flight. Not sure I can handle your bad food mixed with sand and fish slime right now."

"Your choice, but I'm telling you I only serve the best of fresh fish slime, lightly salted." He pours coffee into an extra metal cup I have. We looked at each other, he is nervous, hesitant about something.

"Damn it's good to see you, Frank. I know you didn't come out here just for the coffee, although it is good enough to travel for. So what brought you all this way?"

"It's good to see you too, Matt. But you're right. It's my brother, Chuck, my youngest brother. He went for a weekend hike, two weeks ago, and has not returned. It's not like him at all. He's a physical fitness guy. Runs marathons, triathlons, lifts weights, and goes for weekend hikes on the Appalachian Trail, three or four times a year. He lives in Virginia so the trail is close to him. He is smart, careful, and tough. The family is worried, we just don't know what could have happened to him. The police were notified, but it seems there is little they can do for a missing person. We put signs with his picture near the part of the Appalachian Trail he was headed for and posted a reward. Search parties have gone out twice now looking for any sign. All of that has come to nothing.

I told my parents and sister-in-law about the way you seemed to get into the head of Jenny's killer and how you found her just by sitting on that river bank and thinking where she would go. Matt, I think you are our best chance to find him. My family agrees with me and asked me to contact you. We have collected a little money to give you if you will help. And we desperately need your help. We don't know where else to go."

I have been busy making breakfast while listening to him. Two eggs and cut-up sourdough bread chunks fried in butter, and coffee, lots of coffee. I dump the eggs onto a paper plate and offer half to Frank, but he just shakes his head.

I begin stuffing food into my mouth. "Frank, I will help you anyway I can, but you gotta know I'm no hiker and I don't know diddly about the Appalachian Trail. I'm not sure that I can do anything that hasn't already been done. You know we got lucky when we caught the last one. We used a lot of luck and guessing to arrive at where she would be. Still we did get her. That was so great." I toss the rest of my breakfast mess into the fire and begin working on the coffee.

"Sure would be obliged if you would try." A funny expression comes over his face, "Seems I got a ton more faith in you than you got in yourself."

I reach into my tent, get a bottle of Jack, add a healthy slug to both cups of coffee. "Help me tear this camping crap down and we'll be off. Long as you understand you gotta help me, I'm in. And just so you know, I will find him. I have complete confidence that we can find him. I just hope we find him in time. You got a car near here so we don't have to walk? If he has been out there two weeks, we got no time to lose."

Everything is damp and sandy as we pack it. Have to dry and clean it later. We are on our way within thirty minutes and by one o'clock we are strolling through the huge glass doors of the Seattle airport. Frank obviously knew he would get me to help because he had purchased tickets before coming to see me. Purchasing an extra ticket is not in Frank's wheelhouse. He is not so much very frugal as downright cheap. We have extra time as the flight is scheduled for three twenty, so I order up a medium rare rib eye steak and a glass of the local wheat ale, trying to get the taste of that sourdough bread mess out of my mouth. I really need a shower but that will have to wait. Let the other passengers sit at a distance. At a store in the airport, I buy a Guide to the Appalachian Trail book. Better find out what I am tackling. We are in the air before I think to ask Frank where we are going.

"BWI, just outside Washington, D.C. Chuck went on to the trail just north of The George Washington National Forest. I thought you would want to start there, where he went in. I'll go with you to help."

"Tell me about Chuck."

"He's really a stand-up guy, twenty nine, married with three kids, two little boys he dotes on, and a daughter who is the star in his heaven, happily married from all I can see. He earns a good living. He's a stock consultant with a small brokerage, no problems at work. Very congenial. The life of the party type, everyone likes him. Seldom has more than one drink, strong, healthy. He plays softball all summer on a top team and he golfs, although he is not so good at that. He told me once that he uses the trips on the Trail for self time where he can be alone with his thoughts.

"How's his wife doing?"

I think she's holding up pretty good. She is a cutie he met in his first year at college and they have been solid ever since. Turns out she is a strong-minded, iron-willed little cutie. She's always busy with something. She's a good cook and her house is always pretty clean. With two young boys and a daughter running around, it's never immaculate. It always has that nice lived in quality. The boys take up much of her time, running to one sport or another. She works part time as a yoga instructor. She does the girly stuff too, scrap booking, needlepoint, that type of stuff. She is a nice lady, I like her a lot."

"Give me a few minutes to cogitate here, Frank, then we talk."

I close my eyes and try to move my aircraft's seat-belted torture chamber to the recline position. Give that up quickly and just sit with my eyes closed.

Roughly ten minutes later, Frank gives me an elbow. Opening

my eyes slightly I see a beautiful sight. The flight attendant is coming down the aisle with the drink cart. We both have a bourbon and water.

"You know I envy you your police training. My training is all self-taught from my escape back in Vietnam. I had to figure out where I could safely travel by watching the people and the animals. The more I watched and learned to understand their patterns of life, the easier it became for me. So between us, maybe we can figure this out. Let me know if you think I am off base. So you want to know my plans and what I'm thinking now. Or would you prefer to just hit the trail at the jump and see what happens? I don't want to worry you if I don't need to, so you decide."

Frank sits quietly for another twenty minutes and then "Tell me. And what you tell me will stay with me. That way we can bounce ideas off each other. If you get too far out, I will let you know."

"Okay, well, here goes. I trust your assessment of your brother. If he has some huge character flaw, I believe you would have told me because you really do want to find him. I'm going on what you told me. By that I mean, I wouldn't expect to find him in some casino in Vegas with a showgirl."

"I see three possibilities. First, he could be dead. He could have had a fatal accident falling off The Trail, or been attacked and killed by someone or something. If that is the case, we will find him, but it may take longer and there is no hurry. Second, he could have been abducted and is being held for ransom. Since he works at a brokerage firm, that is a possibility. He may be working with some huge sum of money that has made him a target. But I would think they would already have contacted the family for ransom. We'll totally ignore the first two, at least for right now. We are going on the supposition that he has had an accident. Something forced him off the Trail and he was injured. Severely enough that he could not return to the Trail so the injury is probably to his legs or his back. If he has had an accident, then something could have happened to his phone or he is in an area where there is no reception. I am hoping he has enough food in his pack and that he was able to get to a source of water. I want you to understand that before I get started. What I think we need to do is to find the right section of the Trail and search there diligently. We will have to look past the obvious places as they have already been checked.

"Tomorrow, we buy two cell phones, good enough so that we can talk while we are on the Trail. We should carry walkie-talkies just in case we find an area with no reception. We will need a week's supply of food, good quality maps of the area where he started, two sets, one for each of us, and two hundred miles in each direction. I doubt he went that far but better to have too much map than too little. The phone should come with a GPS function but if there is no reception, we will have to use the maps. The maps will also include legends and topography that may not be on the GPS. Besides, I am old school and like maps. Then we go to where he entered and I begin searching. You can drop me off where he started and I will go by myself. As soon as I find something, I will let you know and you can come meet me. I really do my best stuff when I am alone. No distractions. One more thing, see if your sister-in-law or any other relative who lives here in Virginia can get a gun for us. Don't want to run into trouble and be unarmed."

We get our errands done that night. Drive to a cheap motel near the entry point to the trail. At first light we have breakfast, then Frank drives me up to the drop-off point.

I start up the foothills slowly, it's about ten o'clock. Going to be a long day for me, although the pathways are still paved this low and that make this section easier. I lay in a course as direct as possible from starting point to the trail, thinking that was how Chuck would have gone. Since he was experienced, he would probably try to avoid most of the weekend hikers who frequented the lower paths.

My knife, a K-Bar, is carried around my neck on a lanyard. I use a five foot staff, to aid in walking and for balance. It weighs about a pound and a half. I wear jeans and have a web belt with two canteens attached. This hike is commando, New Balance walking shoes, no socks, tee-shirt with pocket, field jacket for warmth, plastic spoon in shirt pocket, chain around my neck with a small can opener, back pack with food, extra can opener, cigars, lighter, tooth brush and small tooth paste, water purifier, sleeping bag, a one man tent tied to backpack, one hundred and fifty yards of light line to tie the backpack up out of reach of animal scavengers, several dozen zip lock bags- no toilets up here and you need to carry everything out- and phone and maps in pocket of field jacket. Frank has provided me with a 38 caliber police special with five rounds. It's illegal to carry in a National Park, so I keep it hidden in my pack.

By early afternoon a gentle rain begins to fall. The trail is no longer paved so footing is more iffy. I slow down and walk carefully. The temperature is dropping, feels like it is in the forties. By nightfall, still a mile from the Trail itself, I set up camp, eat a cold dinner, tie my food up high in a tree, take my meds and crawl into the tent. I suck down both canteens of water; dehydration is a real concern and both the cold and the rain conceal its effects. Being less than fully hydrated puts stress on the heart, thinking becomes fuzzier, and eyes don't see as clearly. Good to have a zip lock bag in the tent to handle the results of drinking a lot of water because my bad knee makes the chore of getting in and out of a small tent time consuming. The sleeping bag keeps me warm enough. Soon I am sleeping like a beagle by a warm fire.

In the morning, I make instant coffee, eat a couple of oatmeal bars, break down the camp, and I'm off. This entry trail is slow, steep, and winding this high up. I have crossed four rapidly moving creeks on log bridges with rope hand holds. Everything is still cold, wet and slippery. Slow...slow...slow... By noon I make the Trail proper. If I have understood Chuck's mind correctly, this is where he began his time on the Appalachian Trail. I sit on a fallen log and light up a cigar. The beauty around me is more than I expected. I believe Chuck hiked south. It's difficult to get into someone's mind and I know so little about Chuck; still I have to make a decision. I would go south, so I think he would go south also. I pray I am right.

I have been walking for approximately eleven hours now. Chuck, being a marathoner, will have gotten to this point in half the time by my estimation. Since he also started in the morning. I expect he would have passed this place before camping on his first night. If he was injured on the trail, he would have stayed on the trail and been found by now. If he was attacked, I should see signs of a struggle. I just have to scrub the trail for any sign of him.

The Trail here is essentially level. Meaning no ladder needed to climb and no butt sliding to go down. All upright walkable. I watch the edges of the trail, look at the trees for fresh marks, if any. Slowly, very slowly, I move south. Not really knowing what I am looking for, hoping I will recognize it when I see it. No trash littering on the trail helps. I keep looking for marks of a fight.

At early afternoon, I stop at a shelter and eat my lunch. Protein bars, with chocolate chips and protein bars plain, yum yum. Nothing like a varied diet. I had filled my canteens back at the creek. Now I drink them both for lunch. Time for a cigar. The only thing I have learned thus far is that physically I am capable to doing this. There is nothing of interest to me, in or around the shelter.

I walk slowly south again. Watching both sides of the trail. Rain has fallen several times in the last week and is falling now so most traces of people passing are gone. I still watch. I walk slowly. Look hard. But there is nothing, I am seeing nothing. I set up early that night. Grab a quick bite, tie up my food, and walk farther ahead on the trail.

I am two miles down from my camp site, its dark now, and I am look over both sides of the trail, trying to see any light. I walk back slowly, looking over one side, then the other. If he is alive, I hope he will be able to show some light, a fire or flashlight. I go through my camp and head up the trail watching both sides again for another mile. I see nothing. Cold, discouraged, tired, I crawl into my tent and pull the sleeping bag over me. I call Frank on the phone, bad reception, but I shout "nothing," and hope he understands me.

I am exhausted. My sleeping bag is my best friend and in the morning, I don't want to get up. Finally, I do get up. I call Frank, tell him where I am, "If you want to come, meet me on the Trail. At this point four eyes are better than two."

"I'm on my way, should be there late tonight or tomorrow."

"Bring some doughnuts, God knows, I need a doughnut." Being a cop, I'm sure he understands.

I eat my bar as I walk. I find now I can set up and break down camp rapidly, growing to hate carrying that backpack though. Routine kicks in immediately and I watch the trail, watch the trees, look for anything out of place, search the shelters, walk a little farther, search the trail, look at the trees. Make an early lunch, hot coffee, Spam, a bagel, a cigar.

"Chuck, what the hell did you do? Did someone attack you at night, was your guard down? Or, did you walk in on something and get blindsided?" I just don't think he had an accident. He would not have left the Trail without marking the place for others to find. Reason begins to tell me there has to be a third person involved in this.

That afternoon I find it. It's a pile of cold sodden leaves which sits in an unnatural place. This high up in the mountains, the wind blows hard. Any storm or change of weather cleans the trail of the many leaves which fall on it. They are pushed to areas where the wind can push them no more, in the lee of rocks, between two large trees or in a hollow of the trail. There is no reason why this pile of leaves would be where it is. This has to be the work of man and therefore, suspicious. I scrape the leaves away carefully and find an old campfire underneath. Now why would someone try to hide a campfire? I use my K-Bar to scrape the ashes and burned sticks away.

They are black, covered with ash, and tiny. I almost miss them. I pick them up and rinse them off. They appear to be very small finger bones. They look to be human finger bones. Realizing that raccoon or opossum bones are much the same size, I continue to dig into the fire's ash. Then I find the skull. It's child size. I am looking at the results of an evil act. I feel the rush of blood. It's small but definitely human.

Fear fills me as it hasn't since I fled from my Vietnamese captors, forty years ago. Those small men had imaginative minds for degrading men by inflicting pain. The constant wetness, no shoes, no clothes, minimal amounts of food for days at a time, leaches, mosquito's, feeling totally helpless in a land where every plant has a thorn and every animal tries to bite you.

Part of the Vietnamese science of warfare was turning their own young men into being less than human. They could bleed evil from the blackest parts of their mind. Then placing the most vicious men in charge of the captive Americans. Most U.S. Combatants recovered and turned from evil. But, forty years later, it lives and rises up in me, leaving me terrified. Perhaps, this is the reason I was allowed to survive the horror and disease this long. I am meant to be the one to oppose and stop this evil.

This is a crime scene. I call Frank and ask him to contact the police. I have found a murder site. I leave my phone on and at the scene so the authorities can locate it with their GPS.

I sit and watch the fire pit. Light a cigar. Look both ways on the trail. Get up and walk about a quarter mile south, then one north. I am sure within myself that this is what happened to Chuck. He was down trail coming back toward his car. He saw someone killing or burning a child. He would have tried to help. So he was overpowered or the child was dead because he left. He must have been running away when he left the trail. I can't think of any other reason for him to leave the trail. And given Frank's assessment of him, he would not let a child be torture or burned if he could stop it. He must have missed a stepped in the dark and became injured in a fall off the Trail. Hopefully he was able to hide before the person or people who had done this to the child came looking for him. I know it's only conjecture, but this seems to be the most reasonable explanation of what could have happened with Chuck. Leaving us with the possibility that he could still be alive.

Therefore, from the fire pit backward, I will search the sides of the mountain. I walk to the edge of the Trail and shout "Chuck, Chuck, can you hear me?" Nothing.

I take my fiberglass line out, the rope I use for food storage. Tie one end to a tree and throw the rest over the left side of the mountain. Work my way slowly down hill using my walking staff, unraveling as I go. When the rope runs out, I am one hundred and fifty yards down. Shout "Chuck, Chuck." Nothing. Work my way first to the right, about one hundred yards, it's slow going in the thick brush on the side of a mountain, keeping track of where the rope is also. I continue to shout for Chuck. Go back to the rope and work my way to the right, search as diligently as I can in the fading afternoon light. Nothing. I go back to camp and set up. Exhausted, I sit and smoke, try to rejuvenate my flagging spirit.

Soon after I get back to camp, the police arrive, Frank is with them. They put up that yellow crime scene tape that they love so much. Thank God, camp is set up far enough up the trail that I won't have to move it. I tell Frank where I have searched over the side of the mountain and suggest that we begin again in the morning. He is way too impatient for that and goes over the right side of the mountain. I can hear him shouting for Chuck.

A little after dark, he returns. The police have left, taking much of the campfire ashes. We start a new fire in a new place. Sit and talk, make plans for the morning. When it is very dark, we walk the trail, a mile each way, trying to spot any fires or lights down the mountain side. Finally, I crawl into my tent and wrap up tight. Sleep, I need sleep.

The next morning, over coffee and donuts, I tell Frank that if Chuck is alive, he's probably down Trail from where we are. “He probably came up the Trail, saw what was happening, went back down the Trail to get the Authorities, went off the side of the Trail to hide and injured himself somehow. We need to look down Trail and near water. If he is alive, he must be near water.

We hike a quarter mile down the Trail, throw the line over the left side and descend to start our search. “Take your time, Frank, shout if you see anything suspicious.” I search to the left of the end of the line, Frank goes right. We work our way out about one hundred yards each way. Find nothing and come back. We chance it and go down another hundred and fifty yards and search again, still nothing.

We work our way back up the mountain. Go over the right side of the mountain this time and begin the same search. My throat is sore from shouting. With each swath we are searching a three hundred by two hundred yard patch. Minuscule when compared with the size of the area he could be in. It is a very tiring procedure. I am not much of a mountain goat, my body is made for easy chairs.

We hike down the trail another quarter mile and begin again. Three hundred yards down, Frank calls to me. “Listen... listen, can you hear water running?”

CHAPTER THREE
CHUCK

"Oh yeah, it does sounds like water, down and to the right." I say.

We go down and begin searching. Frank is quicker at this than me. He goes behind an outcropping of rock and shouts, "here, over here." There is a tiny spring flowing and a man lying next to it. "Chuck, Chuck," he shouts. He rolls the body over and says to me, "It's Chuck and he's alive. He is warm, I can feel a pulse."

I put my jacket under him, use Frank's to cover him. We begin to rub his arms trying to keep his circulation going. His left leg is bent at an odd angle. Easy to see why he is still here.

"Frank, call 911, get some help. Then bring that rope down, while I cut some saplings here to make a stretcher. The faster we can get him up to where a helicopter can pick him up, the better chance he has to survive this."

By the time we get him on the stretcher, Chuck is responsive but not really too coherent. Just babble. But he is alive. All we have to do now is get him a couple of hundred yards up the side of a mountain in the rain, trying not to injure him further. We carry him up the mountain carefully, one yard at a time. Lift, push, set back down. Repeat. But it works and we get him up on the trail in about forty minutes. My arms and legs are on fire from the exertion.

I am surprised by how many police are at the site. When I see the dogs, I think maybe I understand. They believe there are more bodies. An intensive search is underway. It is evident in the demeanor of every policeman that this perpetrator is a man who must be caught. Murdering a child does activate the Authorities. Few things are more heinous to the population and therefore, more dangerous to those politicians who wish to be reelected. Justice must be done.

We ride back to the hospital in the helicopter with Chuck. We both believe he will survive, but sitting in the ER waiting room is always tense. Finally the white coats come with good news, Chuck will survive his ordeal. The bad news is that he will lose part of his leg. The broken bone has shut off the circulation to part of his leg and gangrene is present. Still, he is alive, hard to believe after the time he spent exposed to the elements with a severe injury. He must be tougher than wood pecker lips to have survived that ordeal.

While they prepare Chuck for surgery, Frank telephones the rest of his family. Nothing can be done with Chuck until his wife is here to authorize it. Frank takes a cab out to get the car, while I book us a block of three rooms at a close motel. Once I get all my gear stashed and eat, I head back to the hospital to see how he is doing. His wife has arrived and approved the surgery. Four hours after he goes in for surgery, Frank is allowed into the Recovery Room with him. He has regained consciousness now and he will be allowed to have visitors tomorrow.

We all go out to eat. There is a Denny's half a block down the street from the hospital. Soon, Frank, Chuck's wife, and three kids are munching away. Very little is said. Julie, Chuck's wife, looks tired. The weeks of worry and stress have taken a visible toll. Still, she is kind and thanks me for finding Chuck. Of course, it was truly Frank who found him. The release of all the worry has everyone hungry and tired. They are overjoyed that he is alive. The loss of part of his leg is slight compared with knowing their husband/dad is coming home.

By the time I get to the hospital in the morning, his family has all been in to visit him. I get the news that he lost his left leg above the knee, which is terrible but with the advances made in prosthetic limbs, it is manageable for a strong person with a good support system like Chuck's.

When the family leaves, I slip in for a minute. "Chuck, I'm Matt, one of the men who helped find you. Do you remember anything about this guy? Anything to help me catch him?"

"I remember you from the helicopter, Matt. Thanks for the help. I only saw him for a minute at night. He is a big man – a heavy man. Looked close to seven feet tall, probably three hundred pounds, dirty, black hair, field jacket, jeans, boots. He is crazy, laughing, singing, jumping around the fire. I started to rescue the boy, but I could see he was dead. Nothing I could do for him. If you see his parents, tell them how sorry I am. The man was incredibly strong, but I managed to get away from him and ran back down the Trail. He was burning a boy. My God, why would anyone do that?"

That is all Chuck can tell me about him. I don't think it will help much, but it's all I got. Whoever he is, he will not stay on the Appalachian Trail any longer, too many police watching for him there. I go back to the motel room and study the maps. Where does a monster go when his existence has been revealed and he has been dislodged?

Harry has grown to hate his job. Proud as he had been when he first starting work at the library, now he detests it that much. Eight years of boring, repetitive, work, barely enough pay to cover living expenses, he gets a cost of living every year, but it's never enough to get ahead of expenses. He resents the eight long hours of the mind numbing grind every day, with slight room for advancement. Unless Old Crow McGill retires or quits, he has no where to advance, and she has shown no indication of that ever happening. Hatred continues to grow until the black day when he gets the pink slip, then came despair. What he had hated, now he longs to keep.

At first, his wife is comforting and understanding and he is confident. They both believe he will quickly find a new job, it will be a better job with more pay and benefits. With Harry's education and good work record at the Library, he will have no problem. By the end of the first day, Harry knows this is an uphill climb. Unemployment lines and forms to fill out. The income is a life saver, but the paperwork very time consuming. As the weeks drag by and the stack of unpaid bills grows larger, he can tell his wife is becoming distant to him, very judgmental, like she is blaming him for the library cutting back on personnel. And really, is it his fault the economy is so bad. He keeps telling her about the jobs he has applied for and that he has a good chance to get this one, but his fruitless search for work is exhausting. No one is hiring. He is only thirty four years old, young enough to handle any new job and with a bachelor's degree in English, he could readily adapt to any position. He knows he needs a better suit of clothes and respectable shoes, but where is he going to come up with three to four hundred dollars now. At six foot five inches tall, and weighing three hundred and twenty pounds, Harry knows he does not present the image most small businesses are interested in. Unfortunately, the physical laboring jobs are not hiring. He tries the truck ports, the slaughter houses, airport luggage handlers, anything he can think of that his size would be an asset, but no one is hiring. He begins to hate the employees who watch him from the corners of their eyes with a superior attitude. Even the people walking past him on the sidewalk seem to him to have a better-than-thou air.

A change is gradually coming over him, a new Harry is gradually taking over his actions. He had ripped up his last employment application and thrown the pieces at the smug ass behind the desk. He had screamed at the manager in McDonald's, everyone knows McDonald's is always hiring. Later, he thinks he should have decked that smug asshole. Now, broke and hungry, he is looking at an excellent pair of leather hiking boots in a store window. He doesn't eat lunch any longer, carefully hoarding the tiny amount of cash he still has. Maybe this store needs help. The elderly man who runs the place hardly looks at Harry. “No I don't need help, hardly able to keep the doors open as it is.” The place is dark and dusty.

Harry tells him, “If you had help, cleaned and dusted everything, made it light and bright in here, you would get more business. I will do it for you if you pay me just half of the extra I bring in.”

“Not hiring,” the old man mumbles not even bothering to look up at Harry. “With all these new government regs it will cost too much to keep you on the books.”

Hungry, tired, full of despair, Harry turns to walk away. Changes his mind as he feels a fierce blackness grow, returns to the counter where the old man sits. Hate fills him and without thinking, he grabs the man by the neck with one large strong hand lifts him off the floor and shakes the man until his old body hangs limp. Regaining some control, Harry drops the lifeless lump behind the counter, out of sight. He walks toward the door to leave, then stops and walks back to the counter, around an island in the center of the store. He is struggling to understand what he has done. He has never hurt anyone before. At the counter, he looks over at the lifeless store owner. The old man is lying motionless, a thin stream of saliva is threading from his mouth, he has fouled himself, dirty, stinky and ugly, lying there with his toupee askew. Harry goes back to the door and begins to leave. Again he changes his mind, stays inside and locks the door. Flips the sign around to closed. He rushes into the back of the store to a small sink where his stomach spasms and he loses the little he had for breakfast. He flushes the sink and splashes water over his face. Goes to the shelves, finds the boots in his size and changes into them. Going to the counter, he kicks the lifeless man. "Bastard, bastard, bastard," he shouts, "Why couldn't you listen?" He is filled with an unreasoning hatred for the man, leaning over the body, Harry punches it several times with his fist, then standing, he kicks the man twice more in the face. He puts his old shoes in a box in the middle of the store. Lights the box on fire, then throws six or seven more boxes of shoes onto the blaze.

Opening the money drawer, he takes all the paper money, then throws the tray on the floor and takes the few larger bills that had been stuffed under it. He walks out the back door, down the alley, across the street to a park, where he sits on a cast-metal bench for awhile, watching the store. Then he looks up at the canopy of oaks and maples over his head, glances at the store again, no flames visible yet. The old men sitting in the park near him are looking at him suspiciously. He feels unreal, like time has slipped past unnoticed and not taken him along. He walks over to two men sitting near him, looks at them for a minute. They are nervous. He opens his mouth and roars at them. Like a lion, the inner city king of the beasts, he roars. They grab their stuff and scurry off. "Would she ever understand this?" Harry knows there is no going back. He has changed too much to return to his old life. As he walks away from the park, he feels the weights and shackles of old useless morality drop from him and he feels free as never before. The store is putting out a good amount of smoke now and in the distance, Harry can hear sirens headed toward it.

Getting onto the first bus, he sees it is going east. He rides it to the end of the line, then begins walking eastward. A thumb out results in a ride on a flatbed trailer. The trucker drops him off near the Appalachian Trail the next afternoon. He goes into a second-hand store near the Trail head. He talks to the counter man there and buys what the man recommends. A used sleeping bag, backpack, a belt with canteens and a water purifier, a roll of tape, a small rope, and a knife. He passes on the tent, thinking he can stay at the shelters. He is practically ready now. Three bottles of water, two dozen Snickers, two cartons of cigarettes, and a lighter, and he is up for the challenge of the Appalachian Trail. He had picked up $195 at the shoe store and spent $126 in supplies.

The long hike has fascinated him for years and he read several books about it while he worked at the library. It has been a dream of his for years. He never believed he would have a chance to try it, not while he was still working. Now things have worked out, he is sure he will have no trouble. He begins the hike with confidence and long strides. By the third day, he is ready to quit. Long strides have become short painful steps. His legs and back ache from walking and carrying that god-damn pack. The straps from the pack bite into his shoulders. He has never considered the hard physical exertion needed for a long hike. And the heat, the temperature is setting records along the east coast. He travels from water source to water source. The first week is physically the worst week of his life. He seldom goes more than a few miles per day. He begins to hate Snickers. Cigarettes are running thin. Probably be better for him if he quit anyway. Still, his weight is going down and when he rests, he feels at peace. No wife, no work, no worries, the lack of pressure is life saving. What hikers he does meet all talk to him as an equal. As the hot weather breaks, he begins hiking further each day.

A man joins his campfire late one afternoon. They enjoy a comfortable time talking and drinking a pot of coffee. Then near twilight, Harry goes into the trees to relieve himself and on the way back, clubs the man's head with his staff, easily rendering him unconscious. Harry is quite surprised that he has done it, but the man looked so vulnerable that he couldn't resist. Using a rock, he kills the man. At first he is unsure why. Then he feels his body become infused with the same wild animal joy he feels when he reflects on what he did to the storekeeper. He salvages what gear he wants from the man, takes all his food, the cooking stove, any money he can find, a credit card, then drags the corpse several hundred yards down the mountainside and stashes the body in a hollow area beneath large rocks.

Back at the campsite, he feels ecstatic, his energy surges. He dances manically around the fire, waving his staff and singing nonsensical songs. He feels like going back down the mountain and hitting the body again and again. The death has been too fast, the man did not suffer. The speed of death ruins much of the ecstasy of death for Harry.

Harry has been on the trail for six weeks now. Whenever asked, he is headed south, south to warmth. To those who are inquisitive, he says he just finished with the military and wanted to accomplish this before returning to work. But he avoids people when possible. He is not in the mood to be around anyone. Too much of the time, their constant babbling irritates him. He meets only a few since the latest cold snap left the temperature much lower. The late fall rains have discouraged many. The hikers he meets, usually just pass him by and move on. He frequently thinks about them walking past him heading north. If he turned and struck quickly with his staff, he could easily kill them. They wouldn't stand a chance. Some weekends, he will see day hikers, but not all that many and not all that often. Mostly it is just him and his campfire in the evenings.

This is the best time of the year for hiking. October brought rain and wind, followed quickly by colder weather. The cold has taken care of the bugs. Plus, with the trees having dropped their leaves, the vistas are breathtaking. He wonders how many hikers go through and never realize how far a person can see in the cool mountain air. The spring and summer hikers miss much of this. The absolute best thing about the Trail to Harry is that he feels he is safe up here. No matter what happens, he is impervious to harm. He can just walk out of anything and forage for food if he has to. He dreams frequently of a charred earth apocalyptic event and how he would be the only survivor. There are no prying eyes or police.

Still it is nice to have people in the world, sometimes. He still has at least seventy dollars and a credit card in his pocket. It's time to visit town. He drops off the Trail and goes into the George Washington National Forest. Sturdy self-sufficiency is great but oven fresh pizza and cold beer are damn fine, also. He stocks back up with cigars this time, thinking they will help him quit smoking and will last longer for the money spent. Funny, but he is frugal even with the dead man's credit card. He also gets some potato chips, they are light and he is craving them. Later that night, he notices a noisy irritating bunch of Boy Scouts setting up their camp several blocks from where he is camping.

In the large quiet of the forest, his feeling about the little shits in khakis grows steadily blacker. He goes from a dark disgust into a over-shadowing black hatred covering his longing and anticipation. Late that night, he approaches their camp and waits. A sleepy scout finally walks out of camp to relieve himself. Harry takes him. Gags him, tapes his hands and feet, then carries him, for miles back up the foot hills to the Trail.

The little guy is cute with his uniform on, his eyes wide with fear. The camp fire is just bright enough to show the glistening fear. Harry begins slowly. Undressing the little guy first. He feels the wild anticipation rushing him on. The uniform and the shoes go onto the fire. Harry begins playing with him. His mouth is taped over; Harry holds his nose so he can't breath, watching him squirm. Just before he passes out, the boy's body stiffens out in one big spasm. That's when Harry releases him and takes the tape off his mouth. Soon as the little guy regains consciousness, he starts again. The first time, the little guy fouls himself and urine squirts into the air. Harry cleans him up with a smile. It is going to be a great night.

CHAPTER FIVE
MATT

It's been three days now. I've rested, feasted on tons of good food, and talked to Frank. He is an asset with abilities. He can talk to the police. They have been searching for more than fifty miles in each direction on the Trail. No one meeting our monster's description has been seen. My first instinct is correct. He's left the Appalachian Trail. Where will he go? A hiker would not move north or west at this time of year. It's too cold and wet. Besides, he would be the only one. He would stand out. He's heading east and then south. I drag Frank out for a beer and run my ideas past him. He has that cop intellect that sees things just a little differently than me. He sees all possibilities. My brain looks at the most probable. Most probable to me is that he is going east through D.C. Many people make a good camouflage. I am looking for a tall heavy man. Chuck said seven feet tall, I think the dark and danger make his description suspect. I figure the guy is between six three and six seven. Such a man would have stood out on the Appalachian Trail, in Washington D.C., during Veterans Day weekend, there will be many man fitting that description. He is using the crowds of moving people to hide in. Frank just solidly holds to the position that he could be heading anywhere, and we should wait until he is spotted somewhere.

I will spend a day, at least, searching through D.C., then head east and south if I fail to find him. Frank will help me by monitoring the airways. He's looking for more deaths, or people missing. He will call if he hears anything suspicious. I return the pistol to him as carrying a firearm in the nation's capitol is a felony.

It is still early morning, November 9. Frank has dropped me in front of the Capitol building. Washington DC, a few days before Veterans Day, is crowded. The rumor is that the President is going to join the people reading the names on the Vietnam Memorial Wall. I won't wait around for that. I am here looking for a monster who kills children. The best place to hide can be in plain sight. He may well be here, trying to blending in with the crowd.

I follow the crowd into the sunshine of a gorgeous day. Breakfast is a ham and egg sandwich picked up from a Korean street vendor. Walking west from Union Station is Capitol Plaza, I walk slowly looking for a tall back packer with dark hair. From here, I can look down the length of the Mall all the way to the Lincoln Memorial. The first Smithsonian Museum, on the way to the Wall, is Air and Space. It's the people's favorite and there is always a large crowd around it. I wander through quickly trying to get lucky. Once I am back on the Mall, I see the impossibility of searching everywhere for him. I just walk and scan the passing people, realizing I will be very fortunate to see him.

As I pass by the Washington Monument, a teenage girl asks her mother why the stone on the top part of the Monument is darker than the stone on the bottom.

Her mother says, "I'm sorry, sweetheart, I don't know why."

I jump in to help. "Well, that's how far they lower the Monument down into its silo every night. The darker stone on top stays out and weathers faster, that's why the color is different. It's lowered every night so it won't interfere with airplane travel. The engineer who told me about it said it was quite a feat. It's all done with hydraulics. He said they use the water in the reflecting pool and that it's all connected with underground pipes."

They both look at me in amazement, I keep walking. I probably should have told them that it was caused by the Great Flood of 1913. That's probably more believable.

The Vietnam Wall is still several blocks down the Mall, almost in the shade of Lincoln's Memorial. As a Vietnam veteran, who served three tours, I should have been here earlier to pay my respects. The statues of the three combatants near the left side of the Wall are realistic. I am a little choked up. The people around me seemed to be impressed also, as there is a hushed, almost reverent feeling. I want to see the Wall, but not the names on the Wall. Somehow there is more solace in believing all who were alive when I left, made it safely back to their lives in the States. Perhaps that's why there are few reunions among Vietnam Veterans. There is a crowd here; soon some dignitaries will begin reading the names of the fallen as part of the Veterans Day program. Most of the people are reverent and respectful. Some are noisy, pushing, probably all very important people, in their own minds, here on vacation. They want their picture taken by the Wall like it is a rock star, not a scream of agony from those who gave the last full measure of devotion.

Walking slowly down the edge of the sidewalk, scanning the crowd for him, some lady running past me, bumps into me, and pushes me toward the Wall. "Excuse me'" she says as she runs on. 'Damn', I look and see that which I never wanted to see. One name, I read one name. Damn...Damn. The name I can make out is Charles White, Jr. That was the name of the man who was my replacement. It's a common name. Probably someone else. It couldn't be the son of the surgeon in Omaha.

The guide books are near the edge of the Wall. Maybe they will have a little more information on Charles. Not that it won't be just as terrible whoever this Charles is. I just want to know that it wasn't him. The line is short, but the noisy important people keep pushing ahead of me in line and soon my irritation level is too high. I leave. There is nothing here to see of importance. Those of us who did come back carry our sorrow quietly. The Jane Fondas of the world have always been more respected.

Hiking out of town now seems to make sense. It was a mistake coming here. After living for while on the Appalachian Trail, the crush of people would be as unsettling and overpowering to him as it is to me. In wanting to see the Memorial, I had forgotten that nothing in society is as useless as a soldier after the war is over.

Leaving the city and walking east, I finally hitch a ride with a man going through Annapolis. I stay on my eastern course, walking and hitching, until I catch a ride over the Bay Bridge and head south to Salisbury. It was a nice day while in the sun. All day long it has been in the mid-seventies. Now with the dark comes the cold, clouds gather and soon a light mist begins to fall. I seem to have become a magnet for rain.

With few a bucks left in my pocket, I treat myself to a dumpy motel. This is my second night in a row to say in a motel, getting soft. Shower long and hot, watch television until late in the night and stay in bed as long as possible. The maid is knocking on the door for the third time when I finally rise. Dressing, I'm ready to face what I must do. It is time to stop the rain. The world needs one less evil. First, a late afternoon breakfast at Denny's.

Heading south, I go past a national chain drug store, pause for a moment, then go in. Since it is part of the chain I use, they should have my prescriptions on their computer and I'm running short on all my meds. Soon I will need to see my personal physician and get these prescriptions renewed.

The sky starts to darken by the time the prescriptions are filled. I leave the drug store and begin my hike to a camp ground on the southern edge of town, I'm carrying my back pack and a walking staff. Staffs are a great aide for balance and endurance with us older hikers. Two thin younger men wearing baggy pants, red shirts, and caps, are standing by the street outside the drug store, talking between themselves, smoking, and watching the traffic.

I greet them as I walk past. Just a friendly, "How's thing's." They respond in a similar manner, then at the corner of the building, another young man steps out. He is also dressed in baggy pants, red shirt, and a cap like the other two. This one is holding a knife.

"Hey old-timer, give me your money," he says.

The criminals I have known were for the most part an unintelligent lazy lot. Clearly, it's stupid to attempt a robbery of an older backpacker who has no money. Committing a robbery with a knife escalates the stupidity factor. On a city street, with people standing near, I think, three strikes this guy should be out. There are two witnesses right here. Then finally, the epiphany, they are together. They are here to help him. The red shirts and caps are a uniform of some type. Three gang members against an old guy, perhaps they are smarter than I thought. There is no way they could look at me and see that forty years ago I was a member of the Marines' elite fighting corps. 'Force Recon.' I have slowed a lot, forgot a lot, but I still consider myself a member of the 'Best.' I am an expert with most weapons and very knowledgeable in hand to hand combat.

My Marine Corps Sergeant had, long ago, identified the two types of knife fighters: The Quick and the Dead. I am forty years past being quick, but I am still not dead. I have a weapon that is significantly better than a knife. His knife is stainless steel about eight inches long weighing a couple of ounces, my staff is solid hickory, five feet long weighing about a pound and a half. My staff is a much better weapon than his knife. Preparation, training, and readiness usually decide battles. I am not worried.

I step back, toward the street, mumbling “Please don't hurt me.” I act as if I am in abject terror. Actually, I need a little more separation between Swifty and me.

He is talking menacingly, while he waves his knife back and forth at me, “No sense in getting hurt, Mister. Just give me your money and the medicine and you will not get hurt.” All the time he is talking, he is coming closer to me. When he is at the right distance, I adjust my grip on the staff. I am holding it with two hands, I lean forward for momentum and thrust the head of the staff at the center of his body, which I miss with him moving around and all, but I do manage to nail him in the throat. That heavy chunk of hickory traveling at seventy to eighty miles an hour lands directly on his larynx. His throat snaps backward and his head snaps forward, then backward rapidly. He does a Charlie Chaplin with his feet flying straight out towards me and he crashes hard to the sidewalk. That has to be hard on his hips and back. He drops his knife and grabs for his throat with both hands, trying to breathe through the painful swollen tissues. Meanwhile the two other members of this ferocious trio seem just a little stunned. They look at their fallen comrade. Perhaps wondering 'what the hell went wrong here.' Somewhere along in this robbery, these yahoos should have noticed that I wasn’t afraid of them and that one of their guys was already down. Clearly not good signs for their side of the battle.

Quickly, I slip off my back pack and toss it up against the store wall where it will be out of the way. The weight of it tends to throw me off balance with any quick movement. I turn to face the other gang members, swinging my staff wildly with both hands. I see they are still too far from me to hit, I grasp it in both hands again and watch to see what they are going to do. They have both taken out knives now and are advancing slowly at me. They separate the distance between themselves now, so that I will be unable to watch both of them. I put my back against the wall of the store so they can't move out of my sight.

I am yelling, “Help! Fire!” as loudly as I can.

Swifty, still lying on the sidewalk, has regained the ability to breathe and is struggling to get to his feet. I cannot see any way that would be a good thing for me, so twisting at my hips for speed and leverage, I swing the solid upper knob of the staff, to the right, and feeling like Willy Mays, smash it full on into his face. Blood and teeth shower outward. The force of the blow flips his body over to the right and his head smashes hard onto the sidewalk. He instantly decides not to get to his feet any longer, lays flat out on the sidewalk and remains motionless for the rest of the fight. I like the idea that his face is a permanent reminder for him of his fight tonight. I twist back rapidly to the left, then taking a small step for additional power, I swing the hickory stick rapidly at the head of the man standing closest to me. He dodges backward, ducks and pulls his head to the side trying to avoid the blow, leaving his right leg forward. I change the direction of the blow and with all the force I can generate, drive it into the right side of his right knee. The staff lands with enough energy to fold the knee inward to the left. The knee is one of the body's weakest points and this blow destroys the tendons and ligaments holding it together. The pain must be incredible. He drops to his right side, injuring the knee still further. He is lying on his side holding his knee up against his chest with both hands. Now he decides to help me scream for help.

There is only one red shirted gang member still standing. He lunges at me with his knife while I am still a little off balance from hitting his accomplice. He misses me by inches but that's enough to give me time to recover. I bring the staff up to my chest again in the ready position. He step back, looks at the two men already downed. I glance at the fallen men also. "I don't think you can rely on them to help you anymore," I say. "Hold it down a little there will you, son?" I ask the fallen man holding his knee. Swinging my staff again, I catch him flush on the right temple and he goes over in a heap. That does quiet him right down.

Not worried about the two downed dips now, I advance on the third man who gives ground rapidly, then puts his knife away, turns and begins running. I go back to pick up my back pack. The second guy is starting to raise his head again, I hit him smartly in the mouth with the staff. I suspect he will remember me for the rest of his life, every time he tries to brush his absent teeth or looks in a mirror. Then I swinging my staff over my head, I smash the first guy's kneecap. If he is not so fast, perhaps he can look into a better line of work. He certainly won't be a valued gang member anymore.

I begin walking south as rapidly as I can down the road. I am trying to hitch a ride and looking for a cab also. Nothing. After two blocks of walking, I take out my knife. If they come again, this will help me be ready for them. I stick it in my front waistband under my shirt. Hopefully I am free of trouble, but it's always better to be prepared.

Watching carefully, I see a group of young men gather together three blocks behind me. I stand motionless hoping they won't see me, but they begin to run in my direction. I am walking as fast as I can, but with my bad knee, there is no run. They close rapidly and are almost on me as I pass a city park. I cross the park's playground to enter a public restroom that I see. If I can get into the building, I can hold the door for a time. They will have limited access to me. I know I will tire eventually, but the police may actually show up and help. If they surround me, I will be defeated rapidly.

On the way to the restroom, a dark shadow steps from behind a tree, swinging a staff with both hands and smashes the front gang member, the one holding a pistol, in the face. Before I can turn to help, he has downed three more members and the rest are slowing up. He is using a rapid back and forth motion with his staff that smashes into one after another. The gang members bunched together get in each other's way trying to avoid being hit. I wade into them following the shadow. The damage I inflict is on those already downed. He is cutting a swath through them, while I follow closely in his wake, making sure no one gets back on his feet. I catch up to him quickly, together we advance. They are totally routed. Those who are still standing move backward, not putting up much of a fight. They have assumed a defensive posture. The force he is swinging his staff with is incredible. They run. They have no choice, they flee the scene. Those who are unable to leave, suffer a few more lumps as we register our displeasure with their former actions. They will all have nice facial scars to remember me by. It's a form of immortality. Long after I am dead, they will look into a mirror, see the scar, and remember the bastard who gave it to them. If I'm lucky, they may even tell their kids about me.

When our skirmish is finished, five gang members are unconscious. The others have fled. We recover five knives, three machetes, a cell phone, and one pistol. The pistol is a 38 special. It's fully loaded and we find five more rounds in the pocket of the former owner. I slip the pistol into my pocket. We were lucky the front guy had the pistol and was the first downed. I'm pleased as a politician with a baby to kiss looking over the bleeding gang members, but am a little surprised that no alarm has been raised with the police during all this. Calling 911, I request an ambulance for the five injured gang members.

The stranger and I grab our packs, our plunder, and walk to the dark side of the park. The far side away from the main street lights is safer. We watch the police and an ambulance come roaring up to help the injured. Soon there are all kinds of flashing lights and at least ten emergency vehicles, forty people running around. Yellow crime tape is blowing in the evening breeze.

I light a cigar and offer big man one, “Hi, I'm Matt, thanks for the help. Your surprise appearance and wonderful use of that staff probably saved my life.”

Tall, quiet, and thank God he was here, takes the cigar, lights it with a match, which he blows out, then throws away. “I'm Harry. I saw you tussling with them dudes up at the drug store. I was just looking to sleep here in the park for the night when I heard you. I still haven't seen that fire you kept shouting about. Looked like you were doing okay though, so I didn't come up. But I'm glad I could help here at the park. I hate those street gangs. You did really good with the first three but you're right, there might have been a passel too many for you with that second group.”

“No one was coming to 'help,' so I figured 'fire' would draw a bigger crowd.”

We smoke and look at each other. He is big, probably two hundred and eighty to three hundred pounds and six foot five. His hair is wild and blowing in the breeze, he looks like the personification of the devil himself. Truth is, I don't really care what my hero looks like, he saved my life. I am sure of it.

“We gotta get outta here while the police and ambulances are busy over there,” I tell him.

“The Police take us in we’re in deep trouble. If they get us, don’t admit anything. Also, that gang is going to come back when the Cops leave. They will probably show up in cars and have a few automatic weapons. I know that's what I would do. If we hurry and are lucky, we might catch a ride. It would be nice to get away from all this without the Police or the gang finding us.

These yahoos always say it's about respect or revenge, but in reality it's all about drugs and money. These are not intelligent people. They are in this life due to their limited ability to earn honest money. The reason that only the very young become gang members is that the young don't have the ability to delay their lust and greed. These are not people who will be redeemed and enter MIT. Their highest aspiration is to be a pimp running a couple of whores. These rascals are dressed in red, baggy clothes, tatted all up with hate symbols, and they were using machetes, how prepared could they be? Sounds like one of the off-shoot gangs of the 15th Street Maniacals. They have a rep for retaliation, no matter what the cost."

CHAPTER SIX
SLING J

Sling J is close to ballistic. As leader of a small associated gang, The Aztekas, his main focus is to keep respect and territory. The area's main street gang is the 15th Street Maniacals. Sling J has carved out a small area to control. He understands that the Maniacals could force him out at any time, but he pays 'tribute,' and he has a force large enough to make his eradication more trouble than any additional money receivable.

Tonight, he has lost seven gang members. He had twenty two members to start with. With fifteen working members, he may be too weak to defend his territory. It's imperative that he present a strong appearance. He also has to deal with the fury of the individual gang members. His members have mistakenly attacked an old man, thinking he would be easy prey. An easy evening of fun and profit has turned dramatically bad. What kind of lame fucking shithead couldn't rob an old man? Now he needs to protect his area and regain the respect they have lost. He keeps eight members with him. He sends six of his more aggressive members out in two squads of three. Each squad has a car and an automatic weapon. Their job is simple. Shoot down the English. Used to call us Anglo's, but English includes everyone who isn't in the gang.

Sling J's mother moved to this area when he was three. She worked long hours at two jobs. He was on the streets early. He began running with the gang at age of eight and jumped into membership at twelve. The initiation into the group was a beating by the gang for fifteen seconds. Hence the name of the gang. It had been tough, costing him the ring finger on his left hand during the violent beating. Now at the age of nineteen, he was tough, shrewd, and dedicated. He had been shot twice, stabbed twice, and spent eighteen months locked up. Until tonight he had not made a major mistake. Tonight his string of luck will become unraveled. Someone has called the 15th Street Maniacals and told them Sling

J's army has been decimated. Tomorrow, Sling J would be dead and his gang would be assimilated. He has been ratted out by a former member of his gang who now drives a taxi and has his allegiance with the 15th Street Manaicals.

CHAPTER SEVEN
MATT

Harry has taken off fast toward the road and south, but I can't walk as fast as he does. Age and exertion have definitely caught up with me and I am fagged. Three blocks down, we manage to hail a cab. We have him take us south of town. I notice the tats on the cabbie's hands and neck and have him let us out on the highway a mile out. Harry has been talking to him all this time, telling him about the members we have disabled. He is slow on picking up my subtle suggestions to be quiet. Danger and fighting can do that to some people, but sometimes, ex-gang members keep in contact with the old gang and I don't want this former member to know what we have done or where we are staying.

"I see your name on the Taxi permit, Mr. Sanchez. I would very much appreciate it if you would not let anyone know where you let us out. I also understand revenge."

I just stand until the cab has turned and driven out of view. I gave him a twenty dollar tip. Perhaps a bribe will work where a threat won't. Then I hoist the back pack up. Lord, I have grown to hate this thing. My shoulders hurt where the straps dig in, my back is always painful, plus now I am tired. There has been too much action today. I trudge patiently behind Harry for several miles.

"This is good Harry," I say.

"Getting a little pooped there, Old Fart?'

"Bite me, Big Guy," I walk up a farmer's cut-away into his field moving slowly to avoid tripping. There is a copse of trees in the field where we will be well hidden from the road. It is a dry camp so no one can see us unless they catch the faint glow of cigars or hear the rustle of candy bars being torn open.

In the small clearing where we sit, I lay out my blanket, no tent tonight, sitting against a tree to prop my back up, I have time to consider Harry. He has been silent a long time. In the dark now, I take out the pistol and hold it down by the side of my leg. Harry has saved my life, he seems to be a great guy, but I don't really know him. He is huge and much faster than me. By the light of his cigarette, I can see he is sitting against a tree also, about ten feet from me. His physical size makes him a candidate for the Appalachian Trail monster. His demeanor and the fact that he saved my life makes me want to believe it's not him. Still. . . I wonder. . .

I come right out and ask him, "Harry, are you the guy I'm looking for?"

He responds instantly. "No, I am not. Sorry Matt but I am straight and always have been. I'm married and love my wife. You will need to keep on looking for your 'special' guy because it definitely isn't me."

I give a short laugh. "That's not really what I meant Harry. I'm straight, too. I like long legs and cute butts, as much as the next guy. I'm a widower, was married for forty years. Tell me about your wife."

"Been with her for fourteen years now– I love that girl with all my heart. Plan on sending her some money as soon as I can. Same old sad story, I guess, as a lot of others in hard economic times. I lost my job with budget cuts at the library. No one hiring for anything. Benefits ran out and she moved in with her parents. I'm out here looking for a place to settle again where I can work and have a home for her again."

"Harry, I wish you the best of luck with that. A man should be able to find a job to support his wife in America. That is the American dream after all is said and done. But what I'm doing out here, Harry, is looking for a killer. I'm trying to catch a man who has murdered a child by burning him. I suspect that he is moving south. I plan on catching him and seeing him locked up for life."

"Damn, Matt, hope you catch him. People like that should be in a cage. I burn dogs and burgers, but only on the 4th of July. I am a librarian who spends a lot of time tutoring kids. Lorraine and I are trying to have a couple of our own. I don't think I could kill anyone, ever, but the idea of killing a child is abhorrent to me. So I am still not your man."

"Had to ask. What kind of work you looking for, Harry?"

"I was a librarian before I got laid off, and I loved that job. Now I will take anything that pays a living wage."

"I know of a good opportunity for you, if you would consider moving further south. A good friend of mine owns and runs

Collector Comics down in Port Saint Lucie, Florida. He just lost his right hand man, Joe. Joe had a run of really bad luck and lost his left knee due to an errant bullet while moonlighting as a bartender. He is at his parent's home in South Dakota while he is recuperating. Keith is looking for a manager to run the store for him. If that sounds like something you would like, I will call him tomorrow."

"Damn, that would be great. I don't know much about comic books, but I have heard of Superman and Spider Man. I learn quick, work hard and I am honest. Right now that would be a dream job. Solid work and living in Florida. Lorraine will be jumping."

His story is plausible. I am at least half way convinced. Still I keep my pistol in my hand as I crawl into my blanket and sleep – sleep is good.

The next day we hitch down about ten miles south of town to a small commercial site with a privacy fence and set up for the night. Traveling and talking to Harry all day has further convinced me that he is not my killer. He is a pleasant traveling companion. We share a pizza for lunch/dinner. There are at least fifty other tents set up so I feel safe, and retire early. In the morning, I start my fire early. Get the coffee going first, basic rule of life. I make my favorite camping breakfast, a can of corned beef hash spread on the bottom of the pan, the direct heat of the fire usually caramelizes the bottom of the hash. I crack four eggs open on top of the hash and let them poach there. I have no toast, but there are several bagels in my pack.

Harry sticks his head out from under his blanket, "Coffee?"

"Yep, got her going. Bring your cup and a plate."

Once he's up, I remember how huge this guy is. That gang got away easy last night. Harry could have killed the whole bunch.

We split the hash and eggs, take a bagel, a cup of coffee, and sit at one of the picnic tables spread throughout the park. "This is great chow. I have been on a candy bar and cigarette diet. I feel like I've lost close to 30 pounds this last six weeks. Real food is a treat." He lights up a cigarette and leans back to enjoy his coffee. I light up also. At last, someone who won't give me grief about my cigars.

The morning air is still pretty chilly. Not crisp yet, but the jacket I have on feels really good. I am still wearing jeans. Soon as I get back to Florida, I will be wearing shorts.

We don't talk, just enjoyed the food and the morning. When we get down to coffee, Harry asks, “How long you been out?”

“Been traveling for ten months now. I like it better all the time. Probably need a new tent soon though, this one is getting pretty threadbare.”

“I been doing without a tent,” Harry says, “I got a piece of plastic I use to keep my head dry if it rains. Otherwise, this blanket does it for me. It's that polymer crap that keeps you warm even when it gets wet.”

“Fuck,” I say, “I need the tent to keep warm. Maybe when I get farther south I can toss it. Not yet though.”

“Where you headed next?”

“I'm headed for that island over east with the ponies. I'm not sure if it's Assateague or Chincoteague. Always wanted to look at those ponies. Heard they swam ashore when a pirate ship went down a couple of hundred years ago. They've been living there on the islands ever since. Just think, wild horses on the east coast, close to a hundred million people living within two hundred miles and the horses are still living free. Too cool in today's world. How about you?”

“I am hoping you were serious about calling your friend about that job. If I can get the job, I will head down there”, Harry says. “I figure it will take about a week to get there. Ask your friend if that would be soon enough?”

“Hell yes, I'm serious. I will call him right now. Come on up to the office with me in case he has any questions to ask.”

Keith is pretty surprised by the call from me out of left field. Still that's the way it is with close friends. I met him at a comic convention back before they became big business. At the time, we were the only adults there who didn't have at least one child in tow for camouflage. Once I found his brain was as warped as mine I had a life long friend. I had thought I was the comic expert of all time, but I had to bow to his superior knowledge.

He still has the job available. “I need someone, Matt, but don't saddle me with someone with no personality. You know this job takes a talker.”

“I think he will be great Keith. Here, you talk to him. See what you think.” I hand the phone to Harry and go to take a shower. It's up to him if he wants it, he'll have to sell himself to Keith.

He is bubbling when I come back to the tent site. “He promised me the job. Said he'd hold it for two weeks. The pay sounds okay. Keith said if I increased business, my pay would reflect it. This is the start of a whole new life for me. Thank you so much, Matt.”

“Trust me, you'll like Keith, he's a straight shooter, but he loves to tell old jokes, really bad jokes, and then he laughs at them. They are so corny, sometimes you have to laugh with him. Why don't you come over to Assateague with me? Its east of here and somewhat on your way. I will be heading south from there in a week myself. We'll easily be in Port Saint Lucie within two weeks.”

CHAPTER EIGHT
MATT

The sun is high before I leave the Salisbury Campground. As usual, there are a few campers still in the RV park. In my tent, I could hear the big diesel rigs rumble in long after dark. They begin warming their motors up again, early in the morning, while it's still dark out. When I poke my head out on the tent at eight o'clock, most of them are gone. I wonder about the vacationers that spend all day on the road. Seems like more work than vacation to me. The small pine trees planted thickly through the campground provide no shade but spread the subtle perfume of clean air throughout the camp. I had broken down my tent earlier and turned it bottom up to dry in the warm morning breeze. I open up my sleeping bag and hang it on the clotheslines behind the office to air out. I shake, and sweep the sand I am still packing from Washington State. I stop at the laundromat in the bathhouse to see if any machines are open. The newspaper in the laundromat has headlines about the gang war fought two days ago in Salisbury. Good news indeed, they will not be looking for me and Harry.

I use the washers and dryers to freshen up my clothes. They definitely need it; my pack is getting strong enough to hike itself down the road. No sorting with camping clothes, they are all drab brown. By early afternoon, I have repacked everything and am ready to go. Harry's sleeping pad and back pack are still here. When I leave, I put a short goodbye note on his gear, telling him I will see him at Assateague or Port Saint Lucie. We had discussed traveling together but it's easier and faster to hitch single. Drivers pick up lone travelers much quicker than two people hitching together.

I hike out to the highway and throw out my thumb. People as a general rule are very nice about giving rides, but today is slow and I catch nothing for the first hour. By then I have hiked five miles down the road to the town of Princess Anne, a very small village with a friendly looking restaurant. There are only two booths inside, and four stools at a short counter. Two locals are sitting enjoying a late morning coffee. I order up a bacon and egg sandwich with coffee to go. I get a little grumbling about late breakfasts from the waitress, but the cook shouts out from the kitchen that it will not be a problem. I leave an extra two dollar tip and carry my food across the road to a small park where I can stretch out and relax while I eat. I savor my coffee. Sit in the park for awhile. Smoke an early cigar, all the while lost in thought. I had been married when I went to Vietnam, but that marriage was annulled. We had never lived together or been in love. I married her as part of the need to have someone care if I lived or died during my time in Vietnam. Four years after I left the service, I met Anne and fell headlong into the one love of my life. I teased her that she was born a Princess and would always be the Queen of my heart. She is and always will be my little Celie Anne. We had often talked about visiting this little town, since it was obviously named for her. We lived less than two hundred miles from here during our working years and never made it over. We were going to live forever then and believed we had lots of time for everything. The stupidity of youth caught us. Damn, sure wish we had come to visit ten years ago. Sure wish she could be with me now, if only to hold her hand for ten more minutes. We passed so many days just living when we should have been busy treasuring each moment together.

Back on the road after my short break, I snag a ride with an older man who has a real talker on. He takes me all the way over to Assateague Island. The more he talks, the more I am sure that he wants to drop whatever it is that he is going to do now and come camping with me. He goes out of his way and drops me less than half a mile from the Wildlife Refuge Camping Ground.

The manager of the camp ground is a younger man in his late fifties with salt and pepper hair, a face showing the lines of an outdoor life. He is reluctant to rent to a tenter in November. "It's too cold out by the beach. If you want to rent for the week, you have to use a space closer to the office. With the wind and rain this time of year it's just safer." What he actually means is that he believes it's too dangerous for an older man to camp in colder weather.

I assure him I am an experienced back packer used to winter

weather. Finally though, it's just not worth arguing about. He is not going to change his mind. I take the site he wants to assign me. Why he thinks a closer site is safer is nonsensical to me.

Once he jumps over that hurdle, he turns almost congenial. Spends twenty minutes telling me about the wild horses. His favorite is a colt born this year that he calls Smokey. He likes the colt because of his dark bluish color like the colt in the novel about the wild horses of Assateague. He drags out a photograph book with hundreds of pictures and starts showing me the ones he loves. Each picture has a story for him and it's obvious that he loves the area.

He changes his tune a little, "I've been getting more business than usual because of the people now who are leaving the Appalachian Trail. There is that strange trouble over there. They have identified the remains of one young boy, turns out he was a scout. The police and FBI are scouring the area, even using the hounds. They have already found three bodies now, in addition to the Boy Scout. I'm guessing some psycho killer was going wild and stashing bodies on the trail. What in the hell goes through their minds? Four dead people for nothing. Seems like there are more crazies in the world all the time. They put out all these movies now about a zombie apocalypse. I think if there ever are zombies, they better watch out for the crazies. Maybe it's the global warming driving these rascals around the bend.

"Have you heard that they found one guy who was severely injured, but is still alive? I guess he got away from the killer. He is some lucky bastard. It's really bad for all of us businesses when that shit happens. I hope they catch this whacked fucking mofo fast. The rumor I heard is that he has been burning them while they are still alive. Sure hope it's only a rumor. What kind of human being could do that?"

"I know, seeing stranger crap out there all the time."

"Well," he says, "I hope they don't catch him here, mad as everyone is, they'd probably hang him or just tear him apart before the cops could get here to save his sorry ass."

I buy some wood for a camp fire, hot dog makings, couple of cans of pork with beans, and a six pack of beer. "Check you out later," I tell him.

The tenting area where he put me consists of a small patch of grass, a fire ring, a picnic table, all only fifteen yards from the bathhouse. Oh Joy-Oh Joy! Lights and traffic all night, with just the freshest hit of urine, blowing with the breeze. I dump my gear and sit at the picnic table.

What the manager said has hit me hard. I thought the AT killer had only murdered a boy. Now it seems he is a serial killer with an agenda of pain. Three murders, then a killing with torture indicates to me that he is evolving. I need to contact Frank for more information, but it seems I'm looking for a worse monster than I thought.

I walk back up to the office, get change and call Chuck's house for Frank.

"Frank, I heard today that there were three more bodies on the Trail."

"Yes. They were all up Trail from where we found Chuck. The theory the police are discussing is that he was moving south and killing at least one person weekly. Not much more information than that. I think you are right, he's moving south. Keep alert."

Since, I plan on being here at least a two days, I set up the tent with a few extra stakes. The wind is always blowing here, off shore and then back on shore. The tent ropes never stop flapping. I start a fire, spread my sleeping bag out in the tent so it will air a touch, open a beer and relax. Here I am, living tall on fat city beach.

I hope I get to see some ponies.

By the time I finish my first beer, I have three walking through my site. They are small pony-sized horses. They seem to have no fear of man. They nuzzle and push me, looking for food. It is illegal to feed them but I doubt I will get the slammer for a few potato chips. They are beautiful. I do wish they would be polite enough to relieve themselves before coming to visit. My site is beginning to smell a little earthy. Now I understand why there is a shovel and rake hanging on the wall at the shower house. I put them to good use, and help fill the garbage can with the large 'horse' written on it.

I put a couple of wieners on a stick and start roasting them over the fire. Before I can slap mustard on them puppies, two guys walk over to say "hi". I give them both a beer and tell them to help themselves to the dogs and buns. They are after that food and beer like a blue tick hound on a raccoon.

Arnie and Bob are self-described 'life partners.' Bob's the older of the two, probably thirty five, dark brown hair, swarthy coloring, maybe six feet tall and right at two hundred pounds. He has the looks of a high school football player who still works out to keep fit. Arnie is twenty five, light brown hair, big blue eyes, five foot five and about one hundred and twenty pounds. He has a light thin mustache that is obviously a source of pride for him, or else he would shave that ugly thing off. They live north of here at Lees Point, Md. They're congenial young men, beaching it for the weekend. I could have guessed the life partner status from the clothes they are wearing. Flannel shirts, Chinos with sharp creases, and designer running shoes, matching Disney caps with smiling Mickey design.

I light a cigar and relax. “I love this time of year with the cool evening.”

“You got a death wish, Matt?” Says Arnie. “Hot dogs, cigars, and beer. Perhaps some time you should talk to a medical doctor about your life choices.”

“You, my friend, gotta relax a little in life. By the time you get to be my age you will have figured out, like I have, that something down the road is coming to snuff you no matter what you do.” I hold my beer can toward them. “Here's to being a bright light while we're here, cause I hear we are dead for a long. long time when that invisible little flame is extinguished.”

“Arnie is a bright light,” says Bob. “He is starring in a new play put on by a local thespian group. He is on tomorrow night. You ought to come to see him. He will be great.”

As we sit talking, two more couples come over and join us. The Heruth's, Chris and John, are in their sixties. They say they are on their way back home after visiting relatives in Florida. They planned on staying at the island for a day or two and then head to their home in Pennsylvania. The other couple, Anne and Bruce Ramsey, is on their way to New York where Bruce is scheduled to present a paper on the medicinal value of marijuana in the treatment of gunshot wounds. They have driven up from Georgia and want to see the wild ponies also. Camping it seems is great for meeting people and usually they are wonderful generous people. Tonight, I've collected a group of freeloading SOB’s. The beer is almost gone, so I walk over to the office and buy two more six packs. It's the last beer they have in the cooler. I pop the top off one outside the office door and stroll slowly back to the campsite. Two more people have joined us so there's getting to be a bigger crowd than I like. Besides, Bob has a shrill laugh that's getting on my nerves. I try to drink another beer and schmooze, but I am at the time of the night when I really don't care what anyone else is saying. It's been a long day. Getting cold out. I crawl into my tent and wrap up in the sleeping bag. Soon after I leave, the people disperse and quiet fills the air. I crash.

The next morning, I am a little surprised to see that Harry has shown up at the camp ground. When he hadn't made it the night before, I thought he had probably decided to go straight on through to Florida. It's always nice to see a friendly face.

“Harry,” I say, “welcome to the island. “Come on, I'll introduce you around.”

Bob has coffee made. I get some doughnuts at the office and soon we have a pretty good group again. Chris Heruth wanders over with a pan full of scrambled eggs, with onions and spam. We all load up on her great cooking and stand around talking. Harry attacks the egg scramble with a vengeance. He finishes off what is left over, now that we all have eaten. Chris and her husband, John have been traveling for the last two weeks and are heading home today. John is not the talker Chris is, but he seems interested in everyone and stands around the group listening. Poor Bob keeps making pot after pot of coffee. I like him when he is not laughing.

Bob tells everyone that Arnie has a meaty role in the play his troupe is performing. Arnie's play is on tonight and he is inviting everyone to come to it. He says Arnie is gaining confidence and is being rewarded with bigger roles. “I can't see him as a Laurence, seducer of women and Wall Street Broker extraordinary. But it's a nice role for him and he should be really good at it.” We all agree that would be nice and plan on leaving that evening about seven. Chris breaks out a Trivial Pursuit game, 25th edition, and soon we have a spirited game going.

Harry doesn't seem all that comfortable around the other campers. He is taciturn and retiring. It is very noticeable because of his size. He's like a silent monolith standing there. He hangs for a short while with us, “Think I'll take a look around,” and off he goes. Damn, I am hoping he is more personable when he gets down to Keith's.

I hike about on the island later in the morning. I fire up my fishing gear and head down to catch me some dinner. In most places, ocean fishing is legal without a license, but here in Maryland it's not. I should have checked. Sure as the one black cloud on a sunny day, a Park Ranger shows up and checks me for the license that I don't have.

He quotes my favorite stupid thing to say, "Ignorance of the law is no excuse." And he says it with a special pride like he's the genius who wrote it.

"I'm not looking for an excuse, write the damn ticket and leave me alone."

"Sir, there is no ticket, Sir." I know I am in deep doo-doo when he begins with 'sir'. "You are going to have to come to town with me to see the Constable." He takes me into town in the back seat of an older Ford Explorer with Park Ranger, State of Maryland, written on the sides, leads me up to the second floor of the courthouse. "Sir, would you please sit on the bench there." Not a question, a direction. An hour later I am in front of a tall walnut desk with a formidable looking man sitting behind it. He is the Constable. I didn't even know there were Constables anymore.

"Got anything to say for yourself?"

"I'm sorry, sir, I didn't realize I needed a fishing license for the ocean. Disabled Veterans and anyone past the age of 65 don't need one in Florida." I show him my Disabled Veterans Golden Eagle Pass. The Constable says to me. "Don't see any reason you shouldn't be able to fish anywhere in this state. Not after the service you provided for our Country. Bailiff, write this man out a permanent lifetime fishing license for the State of Maryland and sign my name on it." Then he says, "How much do they charge you to stay at that Park?" I tell him. "Bailiff, you write this man out a permanent lifetime permit to camp at all state and national parks in the State of Maryland. Anything else I can help you with, Sir? Please take my gratitude with you for your service to the USA." Then he winks at me, "I know the Nationals might not recognize that pass, but you won't be hurt any trying it.

I have decided that Constables are important and they need much more recognition for the service they provide. The Park Ranger doesn't say anything to me on the way back to the shore.

As I get out of the car, I thank him for his service, “It's the work of you and your fellow Rangers that keeps our parks beautiful and safe.” I'm not sure he believes me. I am fishing again within the hour.

Working on this as a good story to tell around the fire that evening, I'm surprised that no one is around when I get back. Few things hurt as much as a good story sitting there untold. I cook up the mullets I caught, in butter and lemon. They are wonderful. This may be the best tasting fish ever. Then I relax, wait for the evening to unfold. Harry returns to camp at six. He is mellow. I wonder if he scored some pot. “Great island,” he says. “I walked way down the beach. This area is incredible. “

“Did you take your boots off and walk in the sand? It's a great place to wade out a little and just wiggle your toes.”

“Nope, just walking and looking. Had to keep a close watch on the horses to make sure they didn't get too close but they are beautiful. Hey, got another cigar on you? I'm running a little short.”

“Sure,” I give him one, take one myself. He pulls out his lighter but it’s not working. I pull out my matches and fire both cigars up. Funny how using matches improves the flavor of the tobacco.

Bob and Arnie shout for everyone who is going to the play to speed it up. “Come on, come on, we need to shake it.” Harry and I ride with Bob and Arnie. The Heruths and Ramseys are coming also. Forty five minutes later, we pull into a church parking lot. The theater is in the basement of the church and seats a couple of hundred people. Arnie leaves for the front of the church, the rest of us group around in back, waiting for the play to start. Mostly they are giving Harry and me the stink eye as we light up our cigars.

When the curtains lift, there are about forty people in the audience. I have never been fond of live performances and tonight's play is the exact reason. Dull story with wooden actors. I watch Bob and applaud when he does. I certainly don't see anything happening on stage that deserves a 'Bravo'. I know Bob is watching with the eyes of love and thinks everything Arnie does and says on stage is wonderful, but for the rest of us, this should be considered inhumane punishment. Finally, half time. In this case, it means half of the sentence is over.

Outside in the fresh air, this time I drink coffee, light another cigar, endure everyone looking at me as if I were a leper, and finally, I wander off looking for the facilities. There are ten women waiting in line. I walk to the front of the church and wander into a small wooded area out of the light where I exercise the male prerogative. Obviously I am well-hidden because as I leave the trees, I see Arnie sharing a hug and enthusiastic kiss with someone who is clearly not Bob. Oh well, true love rarely runs smooth and can really suck.

I walk back to the group, finish my cigar, head back in for another hour of slow torture. AARGG. I hate live theater. I keep what I saw about Arnie to myself. Hopefully for Bob's sake, they can work it out.

Early the next morning, I grab my fishing pole and set off to the ocean to catch some breakfast. I am not good enough to cast into the wind, but this morning the hawk is blowing off shore and I can get the fly out far enough. Lots of good casts but severely under cooperative fish. Thirty minutes later, I stash the fishing gear and head up to the office. I am hungry for pastries and doughnuts anyway.

At the camp site, Bob and Arnie are having a tiff. Harry is still sleeping so I finish my coffee and head off to the beach for a stroll. When I return, everyone is gone. I shower, dress, and head up to the restaurant/bar/pool room for an early beer and a rack or two of pool. I am planning on heading south tomorrow. I am finding that the Fiend of the Trail matters less to me all the time. If I find him, wonderful, if I don't, someone else will sooner or later. Distance and time have reduced the extent of the atrocities in my mind.

I get back to the campsite around six. Harry is working on straightening out his gear. Bob is walking around the campsite. “Anyone seen Arnie yet? Thought he would be back by now.”

Harry and I grunt, “No.”

I suggest, “Let’s go up to the bar and get some chow and a beer.”

Bob decides he is going to wait for Arnie, then the two of them will be come up, Harry says he is short of money until the first of the month, so he will hang at camp.

“Don't worry, I'm fat,” I say, “My treat.”

“I will pay you back, promise.”

"Your credit is good with me. It's not that long ago you saved my life."

It's nice sitting inside with the warmth. It's almost eight o'clock now and the dark brings the cold. We sit at a table, both of us looking at the girl in the bar. There is only one so she gets all of our attention. She is dressed in crumpled soiled jeans that are too big for her. They look baggy and dirty on her. She is wearing a red flannel shirt covered by a worn paisley windbreaker. She has a hat on her head that looks like a squashed mushroom and is much the same color. Small tufts of dark brown hair sticking out from under the hat looking stringy and dirty. She is about thirty to thirty five years old, drinking a beer. Mercy, I think she may be the most beautiful thing I have ever seen.

Silver tongue devil in me pipes up, "Want to join us for a beer and some pizza?"

"No chance, Old-timer, leave me alone."

Harry is obviously as smitten as I, "We have cold beer and an extra large hot pizza. MMM good."

"Piss off."

"Harry," I say, "This lady is just too high society for us. Shall we get another pitcher of beer?"

"Sounds wonderful." He says, "She would have probably put both of us in the hospital, anyway. Great pizza."

He tells me, "I'm planning on leaving early in the morning. Time for me to get my life started again."

"Time for me to shake also. It's been a nice couple of days though. I guess I'll see you down in Port Saint Lucie in a couple of weeks. Hope you love it."

CHAPTER NINE
HARRY AND ARNIE

The change to beach camping turns out to be more puzzling than Harry can believe, walking on sand tires him quickly. The Appalachian Trail has toughened his legs, now it seems like other muscles are being used. The boots, wonderful for hiking on the Trail, suck in the sand. The camping sites set up rapidly, but the wind and mist that blow in from the ocean cover everything with a gentle mist that gradually turns into ą crust overnight. The wind is always blowing, and always carries sand. Sand is stuck to everything. It clings to your skin and somehow sneaks into everything. Getting up in the morning with sand embedded everywhere, especially your hair, is very unpleasant. The salty mist acts like glue causing a lot of irritation on his skin.

Camping on the beach requires a tent, and if he is going to keep camping on a beach he has to get one. With money extremely tight now, that could be a problem, but he is leaving soon, so he should be okay. He goes for a morning shower to get the crust of salt/sand off and feels much better.

He knows he will have to kill Matt one day. In his mind he frequently fights the battle of Matt. He likes Matt. None the less, he has to kill him, but where, and when? He has been awake two nights now wrestling with the problem. The trouble with Matt is that while his is very nice, he is also very perceptive. Harry thought Matt had caught onto him the night of the gang fight. Harry had listened closely to what Matt had said that night. His heart had almost exploded when Matt asked him if 'he was the one.' Luckily, his paranoia had been at high alert and he had known instantly what Matt was talking about. He had been lucky to come up with that I'm not gay crap, but he had to be careful around Matt. He had been able to allay Matt's suspicions with talk of his wife and a job. But he knows his appearance will continue to peak Matt's interest, if he waits too long, Matt will figure it out and reveal him. Besides, Harry believes Matt has a ton of money hidden in his back pack. Matt always has ready cash and plenty of cigars. A good indication of wealth to someone close to flat broke. Harry has faith in his youth and strength, still Matt is a knowledgeable fighter. Something which is always valuable.

Still plenty of time for a quick walk on the beach before leaving. Barefoot and alone, he is going to enjoy a short peaceful walk. He feels better by himself. In truth, he never much cared for the small talk that his former work colleagues or these campers engaged in. Sports left him cold, and he would have rather been reading than talking anyway. Many of his favorite people were characters in books anyway; he had always felt a little Dean Moriartyish. With real people, he has to watch everything he says to keep from telling someone about his great accomplishments. He knows the things he is proudest of would not only land him in jail; most people wouldn't even understand.

The walk yesterday had been relaxing but boring. He is hoping for a little more action today. Walking alone, watching the shore and the ocean, he feels good after that miserable play last night. He feels stupid that he had been talked into going. Still, it is good to build a little more comradeship with Matt. He notices someone else walking toward him along the shore. When the figure on the horizon is closer, Harry sees it is that little guy from the gay couple, the bad actor in the play last night. Harry can't remember his name. Not a bad time or place to meet him. No one is around and he needs a release from the tensions building inside. It will certainly be a unique critique of that ham-bone's acting abilities. Harry chuckles to himself. This might be a perfect time for the park to find the body of one poor drowned little man. No reason for anyone to suspect him. He certainly can use some action and the world will never miss the loss of one little pork chop. But when the time comes, Arnie is not at all like Harry thought he would be. Harry is thinking victim, Arnie is thinking sexual conquest. And Harry receives another type of release.

Harry has always been heterosexual but it had been a while since he had the mind blowing sex with the boy on the Trail. The last couple of weeks with his wife had been too tense for sex. Then there was a long month on the trail before happiness fell into his lap. Clearly once in six weeks was not enough sex. Six times in one week seems like a more reasonable amount. Arnie is here, willing, likes big strong guys and he is always ready for a little action. Harry is at first only compliant, thinking he will snap Arnie's neck later, when Arnie's very vulnerable. Arnie knows his craft, Harry starts to feel wonderful. Indeed great sex, Harry decides, is almost as fulfilling as killing, and as long as Arnie is with him, he knows he can get both. Later, they walk further south on the beach together. Somehow, the kindred spirits have recognized each other and bond immediately. Walking next to Harry, satisfied and proud, Arnie has no idea that he is lucky to be alive.

When they come across, Sam, who has fallen asleep while fishing, further down the coast, Arnie does not seem upset when Harry, pulls his knife and drives it upward into the back of Sam's neck. Poor Sam dies so fast he doesn't even fall from the surf chair. That he has caught no fish this day seems the final sad commentary on the futility what was his life. Little sleep to big sleep. Arnie walks out in the surf to wash the knife while Harry, sat Sam upright with his pole wedged under his arm to look like he is still fishing. Harry also takes Sam's wallet. The two accomplices walk back away from the ocean a couple of hundred yards and sit and wait. Arnie is smart enough not to say anything this whole time.

Arnie is fascinated by the body of the fisherman. He looks the same sitting in his chair. But the universe has been altered. He, Arnie, has been a factor in the changing of the world. Killing a man is so much more than he ever thought it would be. Whatever that man could have done, will no longer be done. He has literally altered the universe. My God, what a rush! He wants sex again. Right then, but he didn't dare approach Harry with that right now. He hasn't been this excited since he held their family cat under water with a canoe paddle until the ugly beast drowned. He had masturbated for weeks on the memory. But this, this is three lines of great coke good. He has found his forever after happiness in this big guy.

Harry's thinking he might have to change his plan about leaving the next day. He can see new possibilities. He says, "Let's head back to camp. We need to establish that we were there for an alibi. We can return later to see who shows up. It's just not as much fun when they die as fast as that fisherman. The next one will be more fun, trust me, Arnie."

CHAPTER TEN
CAROL AND SAM

The first night in the tent the temperature had dropped off rapidly and they had been much colder than they had planned for. Carol had not wanted to go tenting on her honeymoon anyway. Her hair salon was a money maker. She had worked long hours to buy her own business. Now that she was able to afford a better vacation, she didn't want to be camping. She had wanted Paris. During the months they had planned their honeymoon, Sam had worn her resistance down and now here they were. Still she loved Sam and he loved camping. Sam believed that two weeks in a tent on a beach would be a wonderful way for them to develop a deep intimate bond, and to start their lives together. Sam didn't mind the cold. His personality type would wait until the sun came out, then go fishing, the perfect vacation. He made a good living as a mechanic, but he wanted to save enough to buy his own garage. They were marrying late. He was thirty-two and she a little older at thirty-four, but she told him she was just twenty-eight. Both were on their way to being financially secure before the big day. Now they lit their Coleman lantern and Sam put it behind a gallon jug of water, so the headlamp shone into the water. It made a beautiful ambient light. They turned off the light and opened the flaps of the tent near midnight. A deep fog encased them in a world all their own. Disembodied sounds were amplified and otherworldly. Nothing was visible more than six feet from the tent which only seemed to enhance the feeling of solitude. The temperature continued to drop, an unpleasant moist cold. They shared one sleeping bag and pulled Carol's bag over them for warmth. Now the sounds of the waves seemed comforting. Snug and warm, they cuddled and whispered until early in the morning. They slept in late, not leaving their tent until long after the sun had burned the fog away.

The first morning's breakfast was all new to Carol. The camp stove had been left on the picnic table so local animals wouldn't bother it. Sam brought out the cooler with the food and wiped down the table and the bench seats with an older towel he kept for that purpose. Soon he had the coffee boiling and everything looked better with a hot mug of that. Then he did up the eggs and ham. No toast, but they made peanut butter sandwiches as a substitute. It was easier to smile after breakfast. A quick easy clean-up with disposable plates, food put back in the car, and they were off to explore the island. Looking for shells and wading in the ocean, was the perfect way to spend a day of holding hands and being in love.

Late in the afternoon, Sam broke out the fishing gear while Carol read her book in the tent. A wonderful vacation. That first morning, Carol thought maybe Sam was right and this would be a memorable honeymoon.

It had been ten days now. What had seemed fun and endearing now seemed cheap and irritating to Carol. Everything was not as wonderful as planned. Sam had insisted on getting a top of the line tent so it would stand up to the weather. The first night of rain, it leaked on most of the seams, as if it had been put together with cheap tape. Sleeping bags and pillows were soaked and Carol had spent the day in the laundromat. It took days in the sun to dry everything out.

Sam had begun spending more time fishing and less time with her. Sea shells lose their uniqueness rapidly. Carol was tired of the beach, the ocean, sand in everything, boring food, and the isolation of camping in November. Last night she had walked up to the bar and had a few drinks before coming back to the tent and Sam. Sam was sleeping when she returned. He was not the volcanic sexual beast she had hoped for. Mostly he was quick, adequate, and way too concerned about keeping everything clean. He seemed to be afraid of wet and sticky. So it was nice to know other guys would still hit on her.

This evening, Sam is sitting near the shore in his fishing chair. His fishing pole thrust into the vinyl holder and his line is far out into surf. He would stay there all day if she let him. Drinking a six pack of beer and watching a fishing line. His head is off to one side. The boring fool is probably sleeping, dreaming of catching fish.

She walks down to give him a hug and to wake him up. Time they went out to eat. If she offers to pay for it, maybe he will go for a steak. Even a modest warm meal at the camp restaurant would be welcome. That would certainly brighten up her life and might even fire him up a little in his to accurately named sleeping bag. She knows as soon as she touches him. He is cold, in the first stages of rigor. She screams for help and begins running back to her car. Two guys from the camp site come running to help.

"Can I help?" The tall dark guy asks.

"Yes," she cries, "it's Sam! I think he's dead."

"Call 911 right away for an ambulance," the man says.

Now at her car, she opens the front door and pulls the cell phone down from the sun shade over the steering wheel. As she flips open her phone to dial, she notices the man has walked over and now is next to her. His fist is coming right at her face. His first blow throws her body across the front seat. She scrambles across the passenger's seat and tries to open the side door. He grabs her right leg, pulling her back toward him. The second solid blow pushes her deep into the black of unconsciousness.

She travels back from a dark forbidding place to find she cannot move. She is lying on the floor in the cargo compartment of her Ford, her wrists taped together, ankles taped together. Then her arms had been pulled down and her wrists taped to her ankles in front of her, forcing her body into an odd angle, with her face forced downward to look at her feet and her butt protruding sharply. Duct tape is across her mouth. With her head on the car floor, she can only see through the window by looking up. Nothing is visible from her angle but the sky. Terror threatens to overpower her with its grasp. Battling to remain calm, she focuses her vision on a passing cloud. Her stomach and throat burn with acid. If she retches now with her mouth taped, she can easily aspirate it into her lungs and die. Carol does not want to die. Whatever pain and horror they inflict on her, she wants to live through it. Remaining passive seems to be her best option for life.

Carol thinks they will pull her from the Ford when they open the rear gate but they leave her lying where she is. Their actions are very slow and deliberate. They are standing quietly looking at her. She closes her eyes.

"Sure you wouldn't like that beer now?" the tall guy asks.

Harry takes over the action, while Arnie watches. He takes off her shoes first. Her feet have the deep earthy female smell.

Surprising to him that the sex of a person is obvious even from something as common as foot odor. He uses a small knife to cut her jeans from the cuff all the way up her leg to her waist. He is slow and deliberate in his actions, making sure he does not cut her. Blood has that overpowering smell which would detract from the visual feast. He has to crawl into the compartment to pick her up and roll her over to her other side. Her passive weight is heavy. He uses the knife to cut her jeans up to her waist. She has never felt so helpless.

The big guy likes to keep his face close to hers. Almost like he is trying to learn something by looking in her eyes. The little guy is helping now, unbuckling and removing her belt. He slowly pulls the remnants of her jeans off. She still has her bra, shirt and jacket on. But below her waist, only her panties remain. She shivers in the cold morning air.

Harry opens her jacket and blouse. Then cuts off her bra. Her nipples hardened in the cold air. He is very aroused but is too aware of Arnie watching to have intercourse with the woman. He gently caresses her breasts and then suckles for a minute. Somehow, he knows it will be a betrayal to Arnie if he has sex with her.

Strangely, for all the poking, feeling, twisting, and pain they inflict on her, neither of the men actually penetrates her, either vaginally or anally. The strange little bastard has bitten one of her toes almost off. Several hours later, when they have tired of her, the big guy begins talking to her again. “It's getting a little cold, Sweetheart, would you like a fire?”

CHAPTER ELEVEN
MATT

Early the next morning, Bob shakes my tent. "Matt, Matt, Matt, are you awake? The police are here."

I am immediately awake. Have they connected me to the gang fight? Could be bad times coming. I struggle into my clothes and come out, trying to act very causal. Everything is moving slowly anyway. I sit at the picnic table and put my shoes on, feeling rumpled and dirty. So off I go to look for coffee, I need coffee. A totally innocent man would want coffee. There are pastries and coffee, together with the now "usual" group of campers gathered around a picnic table closer to the office. I greet everyone and talk for a minute or two. Then Bob tells me the police are here investigating the murder of one of the tenters. A man named Sam had been murdered the day before. His body was found down on the shore where Sam had been fishing. My anxiety relaxes, but just a little. Now I need to worry about a murder right here in camp. Cops or killers, there seems to always be something to be a little anxious about. I have a pastry, then with coffee in hand, head off for the showers.

Feeling much better, dressed and clean, I approach the crowd around the now-devoid-of-any-pastries picnic table. There are two local police officers asking questions of every one there. Soon, I begin to see that I am being separated from the crowd. More questions are being asked of me, and about my actions on the former day, than are asked of anyone else. I am feeling like a wounded caribou with the wolves closing in. The more they are honing in on me, the more my hackles rise. Although I am not worried about being accused of the murder of the tenter, I worry that if they spend too much time investigating me, something will connect me to the gang deaths. So, the more suspicious they become of me, the more circumspect I become with my answers. They are out to get me! I turn into a monosyllabic answering machine.

"Where were you here on the island yesterday?"

"Yes."

"Where on the Island?"

"Here."

"What were you doing yesterday?"

"Tenting."

"Did you leave this area?"

"No."

"Was anyone with you?"

"No."

"You are the only one of the campers here at the park with no one to verify his story with anyone. That seems suspicious to me."

They were both looking at me. The shorter grumpy one said, "Answer the question."

"What question?"

"Why are you the only one here with no one to back up your story?"

"I was alone."

"I think we should take you down town for questioning."

"I can understand why that would make sense to you. Seems to be a more productive use of your time than actually doing a little police work and trying to figure out who committed the crime."

"Did you know the man who was killed?"

"No, not well anyway. I saw him walking through the campground several times and have talked to him a little. Do you have a picture of him? Then I could tell you for sure."

They show me a picture of the man. His tent was three down the line from mine. I remember admiring his tent.

"I do recognize him. I talked to him yesterday for a few minutes about his tent. His tent is a very nice new one, close to mine." I turn to show them his tent, but it's gone. "His tent was there, yesterday. There in that empty place."

They left me. Went to where the tent had been, took pictures, walked back to me.

"Can we examine your back pack?"

"No. I won't let you look in my tent either."

"Are you hiding something?"

"Yes, my dirty underwear."

"We are not looking for dirty underwear."

"That's good. Because you will need a search warrant to look at mine."

Detective Grumpus says, "Why are you trying to slow down this investigation?"

"I'm not trying to slow down your investigation. I am trying to slow down the train you want to run me over with. I would much prefer that you save your resources and solve it fast. With that in mind, I'm going to give you a few clues. I know you are not detectives yet, but you should still appreciate a clue. Clue number one is: I am not the person you are looking for. Clue two: the dead man was married, but his wife isn't here. It could just be possible that she knows what happened. Watch out now because I am going to really rock you. Here is the third clue: Their car is missing. He mentioned to me that he could easily carry all his camping gear in the back of his Ford Explorer. Once again, there may be a something in that his wife, his tent, and car are all missing."

One police man, the shorter one, sits down at the picnic table and writes out my statement. At least the essence of it. Then he pushes it across the table at me. "Please sign this."

I sign it.

They leave silently. I feel like dried turkey dung. I am sure they are doing their best and my being a smart ass doesn't help them in anyway. I know the police carry a ton of weight for the money they earn. I just want them to keep away from me and avoid any suspicion on the gangland fight. I feel even worse when they find Carol's body. Her body was six miles up the beach in a remote area.

For the Authorities, this is one of the really bad cases. The barbarity of her death cast an additional pall on the souls of even the most hardened investigator. She had been bound with wire – her wrists were behind her and pulled downward near her ankles. Now there was little left but bare bone held together by wire. Her head and face had not been totally burned. They were able to identify her and could also see that her mouth had been burned into what looked like a permanent scream. The area was sandy with no clear prints anywhere. The location was remote with no witnesses, nothing lying around, no additional evidence. A good crime scene for the perps.

It had been a Park Ranger who found the body of the wife although he hadn't realized it was a human in the fire pit when he first found it. He had seen crows swarming near the shore and walked over. At first he had thought someone had dropped a large fish in the fire pit, then he thought a burned dog or perhaps a small pony. When he saw and recognized the partial face, he had been violently ill. He dialed 911. The Authorities had taped off the area, removed the remains, issued a bulletin for the car, and returned to the campground to gather any further belongings of the deceased couple.

All of their camping gear was missing, but Sam's fishing stuff was still there. They asked around amongst the tenters, but no one had noticed who had taken Sam and Carol's gear. They did write down the names for the two men who were also missing from camp: Harry and Arnie.

Harry's gear is gone. I am not surprised that he has gone. Not after he told me he was planning on leaving in the morning. Also, I know he misses his wife and wants to reestablish his home with her. I thought we would see each other again before he left, but I realize when you have financial problems it is hard to take time for a vacation. I hope I will see him further down the road and in my heart, I wish him the best on his new job. Still, something is unsettling to me in his leaving right after two deaths. It's very hard for me to accept that my friend, one who has saved my life, could be a serial killer. I need to talk to Frank. There may be other suspicious deaths. Harry is not the only tall heavy hiker, perhaps I need to expand the area of search.

CHAPTER TWELVE
HARRY

This is his best day ever in his total existence. Harry is euphoric. He tries his best to remain quiet and in control. It is difficult with the power surging through his body. The killing of Sam has been great, radiating intense power between him and Arnie. No pain had been inflicted, instead, the power had come from meeting another soul who understood the joy of the hunt and kill. Sam's death has forged an ethereal grid, locking two together at soul level. His death had been necessary to capture Carol. Harry does his best to remain cautious and filled with quiet purpose. He needs to control Arnie better. The newness of it all is overpowering Arnie and he's practically vibrating with joy.

The time in the car was a prelude. Anticipation built in both he and Arnie. How the electrical charge bursting from them had not exploded the windows out of the car mystified him.

The woman was very strong. Her reaction to pain was not what he had expected. She watched him with flat and emotionless eyes. He had expected hate, cries of pain and rage, maybe disgust, but until the very end she showed nothing. Not just totally blank eyes, more like she had sympathy for him. She seemed not to notice that Arnie was there. No matter what the little dude did, she never took her eyes off Harry, not even a glance. She knew all of the power radiated from him.

The fire peaked the ritual. They put her legs in first to draw out her suffering. The first twenty minutes had been empowering. He became so engorged that he thought about pulling her from the fire to have sex. Her eyes still remained on him, then closed, and just like that she stopped writhing against the bonds. Arnie stuck her in the arm with his knife, but she did not move. Harry knew she was dead when his erection crashed. Only her face showed that she had been in an incredible amount of pain. They spent a long time feeding her inert body into the fire, but the excitement was significantly reduced with her lack of pain. The quick burst of light when her hair caught was the end of the rite. Fortunately for them, the wind was blowing out to sea. Neither the smell nor the smoke drew any attention.

Harry takes her car back to the campground and parks several blocks from the tent site around four a.m. Arnie tears down and loads Sam and Carol's tent and camping gear. Harry quickly collects all his own gear. The two drive off in the stolen car. At the first small gas station, Harry uses Sam's Visa card to fill the car with gas. He hopes the smaller station won't have camera's recording all their customers. He tosses the card out of the window several minutes later. He doesn't want to be caught with their card. He knows they will be looking for the car, but hopes they can use it tonight to get distance. By eight a.m., they have made Kitty Hawk, N.C. They take a short break at McDonald's. Pulling around to the back of the restaurant, they pack up all the equipment they want, discard anything which can be identified as Carol and Sam's, wipe the car down as best they can. Then Harry arranges a small candle with some napkins in the back seat. He rolls the windows down, lights the candle, they saddle up, and hike on down the road, wanting to be at least a mile away when the napkins catch fire. Arnie turns to watch the fire burn the car until it erupts in a ball of flame. His eyes glistening, he trots to catch up with Harry.

CHAPTER THIRTEEN
MATT

Arnie is missing. Bob's running around asking everyone if they have seen him. He's terrified that something has happened to Arnie during the night. Sam and Carol's killer could be near, maybe he has also killed Arnie. Sam and Carol's tent is missing, their car is missing, and no one has seen Arnie. Right away I think Arnie has killed them, stolen their tent, and driven away in their car. He always was a sneaky little shit who looked mean. I feel badly for the two who were killed but Arnie seems so incompetent, the little twerp will be caught quickly. Again, the nagging doubt of Harry tugs at me. I am thinking I need to warn Keith. Harry won't be there for another couple of days, so I still have some time.

The beach and the ponies are wonderful. It is time for me to decide whether I am going to search out the Monster of the Trail, or let it go. I have been wrong about Assateague and Chincoteague Islands, he is not here. Maybe I have lost my feel for where he would be. The way Sam was killed was certainly not like the killing of the Boy Scout on the Appalachian Trail. I have not heard how his wife died, but there no large outcry. If Carol's death had been horrible, I assume an outcry would have been made.

Since the former bodies had been found on the Trail and the police presence forced him to leave the Trail, my belief is that he has come east. East because that is the easiest way to move southward inconspicuously. Traveling down the east coast at the beginning of winter has long been a tradition, with hobo's, bums, beachcombers, and Northerners who dislike the cold. However, the monster, that I am after, might have considered that and traveled west or south to avoid detection. Nothing in conjecture is rock solid, he could be heading anywhere, or holed up somewhere. But if I decide to pursue him further, I will look south, I believe that's the way he is headed. Still, no one has left me in charge of finding him. Now might be a good time to drop it.

My thoughts are interrupted by a low whine. I am standing thirty yards from the shore in the middle of undulating sand dunes. The wind is blowing landward and is kicking up one to two foot white caps. Foam is being deposited on the shore by the wave action and it acts as a border up and down the beach marking the water's edge. I can see nothing moving around me on the beach. I search under the closest structure, the winter-closed lifeguard booth and find a smallish lump of brown squeezed far back under one corner, whining from cold and fear. A puppy has dug enough room to just make it in. It won't come when I call, and with the temperature dropping, I fear it won't survive the night. I coax, whistle, and plead with the little thing but it just looks at me with eyes of terror. Taking off my belt, I run a loop through the buckle, for a makeshift leash. I put half of my pastry down close enough for the pup to smell it. The little one scrambles out for it. I see it is a small male dog. I slip my belt over his head while he munches. He probably hasn't eaten in awhile. His little tummy looks to be good friends with his backbone. I lead and carry him back to my tent, fill my pan with water for him. He takes a quick drink, then finds the other pastry I have put down and quickly snaps it down.

Leaving him in my tent, I head off to the office. At the office/store, I look for any posted signs for a lost dog. There are none. I talk to the manager but he hasn't heard of anyone from the area losing a dog. “Sometimes, people from the cities dump their unwanted dogs out here. I hope the people who drop their dogs out here don't understand how cruel it is to the dog. There is no food for them, little fresh water, and a lot of coyotes which feed on them. There is no way a dog is going to survive on his own on a beach. Here's the thing, Matt. The rules here say no dogs allowed in the campground, but I understand if you need to keep him overnight. Please try to keep him quiet.” I buy three cans of beef stew, tell him that I will leave that afternoon or tomorrow and thank him for relaxing the rule for me. “You might be the break this fella needs, thanks.” He has spent his time trying to dig out of the tent and, in so doing, flung everything in the tent to one side, then buried it all in sand. I open a can of stew, dump it in my pan with the water. He sucks that down faster than Arnie and Bruce had eaten my hot dogs. He circles a couple of times on my sleeping bag, at the place farthest from me, looks warily at me, and goes to sleep. Stupid looking dog is so funny looking he is almost cute.

I am trying to straighten all my gear back out without waking him up, when I hear, the manager shouting that I have a phone call.

"Matt, it's me, Frank, still here in Virginia at Chuck's place. You doing okay down there?"

"I'm feeling good, been relaxing, found a dog, seems like I am on a vacation. How is Chuck doing now? Hope he is back up and recovering."

"Sitting here with Chuck. He's coming along pretty good. Not out running yet but that's cause he's such a lazy turd. Got plenty of good home cooking in him. The pain in his leg is going down a little. He has been fitted with a new leg and will begin working with it next week. Anyway, he asked me to see if you still want that gun of his?"

"I don't know. Damn, wish you were here to talk to, Frank. I've been running this through my mind all day. I may have found a trace of that Monster, but now that Chuck has been rescued, maybe I should quit looking. If I quit looking, I won't need the gun. What I want you to do for me if you would, Frank, is to check out the two murders that happened here this week. Also check around a little and see if any buzz is out there on this guy. Let's find out if I am on the right track."

"I will do that today, Matt. Don't make any decision till I check."

"Can you call me back tomorrow about this time?"

"I'm coming down tonight. Chuck's wife will be coming with me. We will be there about eight o'clock. With this miserable D.C. traffic, it will take us at least that long. I will bring everything I find on the police traffic and we can talk. Catch you at the restaurant about eight. Be nice to see that sorry old mug of yours."

"Be really good to talk to you again also, Frank." I hear the phone click as he hangs up.

I get to the bar a little early and am having a beer, when Bob comes in and slides into the booth across from me. He has given up his search for Arnie, today. Already he has checked with the Actors Group and Arnie's family but no one had seen or heard from him. He tells me, he wants to relax and talk to someone, maybe quit worrying about Arnie for awhile. He orders up a beer. Sits for a few minutes, then challenges me to a game of pool. Hell, I massacre him, of course, he is pitiful and I have no mercy. Before we can start another game going, Frank walks in. Just in time. I am getting overly bored with Bob's continual whine over Arnie. "There is just no where he could have gone. Something must have happened to him. We are always so good together. We have been devoted to each other. His acting is just taking off. . . "I am thinking of telling him about Arnie's indiscretion at the play, but have resisted the urge so far. "Frank, Frank," I shout, "come back here and have a beer with us."

Frank waves to me. Goes to the door, waves to someone out there, then comes back to the bar. "Julie is parking the car. We have an additional surprise. Wait till Julie comes in and she can tell you, it's her idea."

"Sure, let me order up some beer. Will Julie have a beer, do you think?"

"Don't know, but if you order it, it won't go to waste. Wait, better order her a white wine. I don't know why but most women drink it."

We grab a table. He comes and sits next to me on my left hand side. Bartender brings us over some cool frosties. I introduce him to Bob who has pulled up a chair and is sitting on my right side. Ever the opportunist, Bob, has already grabbed one of the beers. Julie comes in and sits across from me.

Julie pushes a bag across the table to me. "Here's the gun. There are two boxes of shells also. We signed a paper saying you can use it as long as you want. And, Chuck and I decided to give you a paper saying you can use our old Jeep. It was mostly Chuck's idea, but I agreed. You know, we appreciate what you did so much, we will always be in your debt. We figure the Jeep will help you with your search. It's parked outside. It's really yours now, but this way we can handle the paper work and insurance until you get settled.

"Frank told us you are thinking of stopping your search for the monster. We understand you are not responsible for catching that bastard, but we hope you continue your search. We think the police will catch him sooner or later, but you will catch him much sooner and save lives. We will help if we can. Chuck has what you might call a vested interest. He says he's one leg up on everyone else. He loves gallows humor. We both have faith in you and this monster needs to be stopped."

I am beginning to answer Julie and Frank when Bob starts talking very loudly at the same time. It's difficult to focus on what's going on. Bob is almost screaming something about someone must be preventing Arnie from returning to him. I am not listening all that closely to him when the night lights up with pain. There is knife is sticking through my right hand, pinning my hand to the table. Bob has my full attention now. He is screaming that he knows I am the person who has killed Arnie.

Twisting, I see he is not threatening me further. He has backed off about three yards and continues to scream at me. "The police know you're the one. You're the one they wanted to take down town for questioning."

Lucky for me, Frank is there and he quickly gets between me and Bob. The bartender is an older woman who looks at us with disbelief. She has an 'I can't believe this is happening' look on her face. She is doing nothing. I ask her for a clean bar towel and a bag of ice.

"First of all, Julie, I will accept your offer of the Jeep and the gun. It is shining of you two to give it to me. Also, please know you have stiffened my resolve to catch this guy. You three have convinced me that I have to continue my search."

"Let's talk for a minute or two then I need to go to the hospital. Don't worry, I'm okay for a couple of minute. Frank, I need to know if you found any action you think looks like the AT monster?"

"We should go to the hospital and get your hand taken care of. Never seen a knife stuck all the way through someone's hand like that. But yes, I think there is and you are sitting on it. That woman who was killed here was torture and burned. Her wrists and ankles were wired together. Sounds like our bad guy to me. I think you nailed where he was going after the Trail. You still got your locator radar going on full power."

"Damn, Damn, Damn. It's that tall guy, Harry. It has to be him. I've been sitting here overlooking the obvious because he is a friend. If this hack at the hospital kills me while stitching up my hand, it's going to be up to you to get him. Kill the hack first, then go kill Harry."

"Not to worry Matt. I'll get them both."

"Now pull that pig sticker out."

He grabs it, pulls it straight up and out of my hand. Blood spurts. The bartender finally comes alive, giving me a dry bar towel which I immediately wrap around my hand. Then I put the bag of ice on top of it, pushing it hard against my chest, I can see the blood is subsiding. The knife is actually a beauty with a good three inch stainless steel blade.

"Carumba!! Bob, you blasted fucking idiot, why did you do that? You better get a grip on yourself, you are acting crazy."

"The police said you were the one who killed, Arnie. I can't let you get away with that. I am not going to let you get away with killing him."

"Bob, what makes you think Arnie is dead? The police didn't say I killed him, they said I didn't have an alibi for that fisherman's death. You and Arnie are friends of mine, why would I kill him. You can let him go, Frank. He really does know I would never hurt Arnie. Now we either have to order another round of drinks, or go to the hospital and get this hand put back together."

On the police report, I say it was an accident that happened cleaning a shark I had caught. Frank and Julie leave soon after we reach the hospital, her children take top billing in this life. The doctor keeps me there in the emergency room most of the night. In the a.m., Bob drives us back to camp in my new used Jeep. I know Bob has been acting out from fear of loneliness and the loss of love. Getting him a criminal record will not have helped him in any way.

"Bob, I am heading south tomorrow. If you want to come and help search for Arnie, I will take you with me. You have to relax a little. We will find him, but it will take time.

"Really? You would help me after last night? I am so sorry I did that. Sometimes I get too obsessive. Hope you can forgive me. I would love to go with you. I'll pay for the gas. OK?"

"Ten tomorrow morning, we're off."

The dog, whom I now have named 'Bogie,' is looking at me expectantly. A little walk in the morning sun feels great. I am rapidly become attached to this mutt. He is certainly not a pure bred and not the cutest dog ever, but he certainly has his moments. He just seems to have love of life that is great to watch. He will stop whatever he is doing and run over to smell a butterfly. Like nothing else in the world matters, but smelling that flying thing. I cover his business up with deep sand. When I pull the cans of stew out he dashes back and forth wildly, almost like he has come to recognize the labels on the cans. I open the first for him. I cannot keep him waiting. Then I have the other. He is not so ravenous now and it looks like he actually eats slow enough to taste it. Perhaps he will turn out to be a good dog for someone. I know I can't keep him and will have to turn him in at one of the no-kill shelters. The traveling life that I lead would not be good for a dog. They should have a little more structure in their life. I will say though, he sure snuggles in good for sleeping.

Bob is fired with the sizzle of sleeplessness and the pain of loss. I can see his plan of finding Arnie is not reality based but I'm not setting him straight just yet. He's doing all the driving as my hand is too swollen. He's a great help. I know he thinks he will see Arnie and they will rush together with a love that has once again blossomed with the force of a nuclear explosion. Arnie will be unable to resist and they will live in blissful happiness forever. But upbeat Bob is driving me crazy. He's singing with the radio, that new horrible music with the nonsensical lyrics, slapping time on the steering wheel with his thumbs, and jumping around in the seat like he is dancing. He is even singing along with some rap shit. I would leave his ass too, if I was Arnie.

We stop at the first gas station to fill-up. Get coffee, dog food, a real leash and collar, pastries, cigars, and bottled water for the trip. I walk Bogie, smoke a cigar. Bob is walking with us.

"Don't worry so much. We will find him. Whatever has happened, we can figure it out amongst us."

Bob has taken another weeks vacation and is a little fearful that he may not have a job when he gets back to Lees Point. Still, he drives along singing, drumming away on the steering wheel, bouncing up and down on the seat in time to the music. This love crap has him wired like he's on intravenous ecstasy. I crawl in the back with Bogie and watch.

We are taking highway 13 south. I watch the side of the road figuring that if Arnie was the person who killed Sam and Carol, he would use their credit card at the first gas station that looked like it did not have surveillance cameras. Then he would toss the card out the window about a half mile to a mile down the road, so he wouldn't be caught with it. He would keep the card in his hand after filling the car, so he wouldn't forget it. He wouldn't want to throw it right away because it would be found too easily, so he would wait at least a half mile.

At the half mile point, I have Bob stop the car. I ask him to stop and wait for me a half mile up the road. I get out with Bogie to walk for the next half mile. I walk Bogie in the grass of the ditch. It has been mown and harvested weeks ago. Now the grass is ankle deep. Not much litter, I can see quite well. A credit card is tiny though when dropped in a ditch. I walk slowly. If I do find it, I will know we are headed the right way. And that Sam's killer came this way.

I have experience in ditch searching. As a money-challenged youth, back in the sixties, I walked the ditches around my hometown searching for soda bottles. Three cent refund seems small but I could make three or four dollars a day. Plus, there was the occasional windfall, like a hub cap, several times dollar bills, and once a billfold, which I returned for a five dollar reward. Now, I just walked slowly, concentrating my watching on the road side embankment. I find the card one hundred yards from where Bob is parked. I pick it up by the edges and slip it into a plastic bag I brought for that purpose. It is Sam's card. I doubt that the police will be able to use it because I had found it. For me, it confirms that he is heading south and that he has filled up with gas here. He will be stopping to refill in approximately three hundred miles. Probably the area that he is going to stay in over night.

Without knowing Arnie all that long, this is at best just a gut feeling that he will prefer to go to the warmth of the south. A tank of gas puts him at the Kitty Hawk, Nags Head area in North Carolina.

I crawl into back seat with Bogie, ask Bob to wake me when we hit North Carolina, and nap off. Bob hums and drums and bounces his way south. I crack the window a few inches so fresh air, heavy with the odor of sea salt, fills the car. The odor soothes me and puts me right to sleep. Just can't take the sailor out of the farm boy.

Bob hits a stop sign, turns to me. “We really are good friends aren't we, Matt? God knows I am sorry about your hand. Sorry to wake you but I just wanted to tell you that I think you are a good guy.”

Damn, I'm thinking this biscuit baker is unraveling fast. This maudlin crap has got to go. “Bob, you need less coffee. Quit with all this worrying. We will find him. Just relax and drive.”

Going through Chesapeake, he pulls over for a hitcher. This guy is a Jesus look-alike, dressed in a brown robe, sandals, which he is not wearing, long black hair hanging past his shoulders and no hat. I immediately dislike like him because of his dress but he is quiet, listens to the crap Bob is shoveling, and he has a box of a dozen doughnuts which he shares. He's heading for some place south of Atlanta to see his mother. The doughnuts force me to change my mind. He is a good guy. Soon we are headed east again and we were traveling through this beautiful eastern sea coast area. The majesty of it rolls out one phenomenal panorama after another.

We pull off at Kitty Hawk and drive through the RV/Tent parks looking for Arnie.

Nothing, no tent, no car, no Arnie. Raoul (Jesus-double) decides we are not traveling fast enough, takes what is left of his box of pastries and departs. Walks away barefooted. Really? Barefooted in today's world. Just silly.

We keep rolling south to Kill Devil Hill. Bob is pretty subdued at this point. “Your blood sugar must be running low, Bob, haven't heard you singing in a while, must be time to eat.” We pulls into a huge 'Breakfast Served All Day' place named Dutch's Diner. This place must hold eighty to a hundred people. They seat us at booth in the far room, next to a large plate glass window.

“Bring us two coffees and two Farmer's breakfasts with eggs over easy and sausage patties, and home fries, please.” I order for Bob, he's still despondent. This up and down mood swing is not endearing me to this losing guy. He is cloud surfing one minute, then trying to crawl out of the Mariana trench the next. Where is the consistent rational thought that allows him to hold a job? Still, the breakfast is perfect. I can see why Dutch's does such a big business. I have my plate polished, including the toast, while Bob is still lingering over his home fries.

"Bob, I am going to walk Bogie. See you outside when you're finished. Don't worry, I got the check."

I am walking slowly to where I parked the Jeep, under the shade of a maple tree, when I hear an engine revving up. I look toward the noise and see a Volkswagen sized vehicle coming rapidly at me. Time stops. I realize I have to protect my left knee. If this car hits my left knee with the prosthesis in it, I will probably lose the leg. I whirl to my right and jump for the curb. The bumper of the Volkswagen catches me mid-calf on my right leg. I swear, I can feel the bone break. I am shouting for help by this time. People come running out of the restaurant, in time to see the small car pull out of the lot and cruise on down the road to the south.

I know my leg is broken. I am unable to get up. The restaurant owner calls 911 for me. Bob is standing with an incredulous look on his face. I know he saw the driver as clearly as I did. Arnie with a joyously malicious look on his face was driving the car. He was trying to kill me. It's just no longer possible to believe that Arnie is an innocent bystander or that he is going back to Lees Point with Bob. The great love and wonderful life, Bob has been looking forward too is never going to happen.

CHAPTER FOURTEEN
NURSE TEDDIE

There are three main nurses providing care for me here in euphemism land. The sign actually says Rocky Mount Rehabilitation Center but it's a nursing home. Late night-early morning, my nurse is GIB (Grouch-In-Blue). She is pear-shaped with gray frazzled hair and a personality as cold as her hands. She smells of horehound candies and latex. Later morning, early afternoon, I get Tiny Tears. Anorexic appearing lady with a pinched-in little face and her hair wrapped into a tight bun. She is always in a hurry. I pick up the odor of lemons and pine sol. I like the late afternoon-early evening shift nurse best. She is pretty, with long gorgeous brunette hair and her whole attitude is different with a quick smile and time to schmooze. She smells of roses and tiny white flower buds. She appears to care about her appearance, while everyone else wears baggy institutional blues, Teddie, of the great hair, either has her clothing tailor-made or she buys her blues two sizes too small. Her posterior moves with an attention-drawing insouciance that gives real joy to a woman appreciating aficionado, such as myself. The half-heels she is wearing emphasize the length of her very shapely legs and add a rolling gait to her movements that is mesmerizing. I know one day, those pants will self-destruct from all the inside action and I want to be here watching when it happens.

"Dear Nurse Teddie, would you be insulted if I sent an appreciative note and a small remuneration to your tailor?"

She has already begun her "How are you feeling this afternoon, sir?" and my remark catches her off guard. She tries to suppress a chuckle.

"You know you have a world class smile, pretty lady, and I'm feeling hopelessly promiscuous this afternoon. How are you feeling?"

"Matt you can't talk to me like that. You're going to get me in trouble." She is laughing, clearly not too upset. "What I mean is, are you in pain?"

"It's the pain of unrequited love that's killing me. Here I am, undressed and already in bed, while you stand there strong-minded resisting all my masculine charms. If you would get me a cane and dance me around the room once or twice I would recover immediately."

"Pain meds?" She's serious now.

"No thanks, I'm okay. A little pain in hand and leg but I can live with it. I do have a real problem you could help me with though, if you can take the time."

"What is it?" She's a little suspicious.

"When I was hauled off to the hospital, my friend took my car to the police station. Bogie was in the car, when my buddy came in to say goodbye, I forgot to ask what he did with my dog. I suspect he put Bogie in the pound. I'll love you forever and mention you in my will if you can find my little guy."

"I can do that, Matt. Let you know if I find anything. And Matt," she winks at me, "I sure wish you had been here when I could have taken advantage of you. You are right, I could have cured you with a dance. "

She comes in later that afternoon to tell me Bogie is in the local pound with a 'do not kill' sign on his kennel. "They are feeding and boarding him for you," she says.

I know she knows I'm watching her butt as she walks out of the room.

Later that day Tiny Tears tells me Teddie is in an unhappy marriage. It's a shame a nice lady like Teddie would have a dick for a husband.

The good times for the day are gone and I'm stuck here for the duration. Few things are as deathly boring as a bed in a physical care facility, usually called nursing homes. My right leg is the trouble. I have a broken fibula, the thin outer bone of my lower leg. I am cast from big toe to New York City. My doctor said a minimum of six weeks at the home. The first day was nice, rest, and three squares. I was still half under anesthesia but I remember Bob came through to say goodbye. Second day was not as nice. I was already rested up and had nothing but television and only the one nurse, Teddie, worth looking at. By the third day, I would have poked out both my eyes if I had to spend one more soul draining hour watching that tube. I had actually forgotten how much I hate it. I begin my evening devotions again: may that God or those Gods which still hold sway with humans devote himself or herself to preventing me from ever having to watch television again.

My doctor wants me to remain flat on my back for at least two weeks and no weight on the leg for at least a month. Through my previous injuries, I have learned to do the opposite. The faster I return to my feet, the faster full use will return. The more pain medications I take now, the greater the pain when I use my leg later. I'm undermining my doctor's orders without appearing to do so.

The heroic mobile library crew came through to save me. I have e e cummings and T. S. and, of course, Walt, for the weekend. Then on Monday afternoon, Dr. Goodbones replaces my long cast with a shorter, big toe to knee cast. I can now climb into a wheelchair and cruise the rehab facility/nursing home. Not only do I have mobility, I can cruise the nursing home helping the nurses if they want any help. Doing something useful is so much better than laying there in bed. I spend a lot of time talking with Teddie and running errands for her.

Eureka, my life is improving.

The first morning in my wheelchair, I can feel the energy start to build throughout the facility. More people are moving and talking. Clearly something big is coming. LUNCHTIME. The high point of the day for many of the inmates. At breakfast, they are still sleepy, at dinner time, they have become sleepy again, but at ten thirty, they are all awake and most, it seems to me, are watching reruns of the Andy Griffith Show.

I can hear televisions being turned off and people are milling about in the hallways on their way to the dining room. By eleven, everyone is seated and the tension is running high. 'What are we going to have?' Meatloaf and mashed potatoes is the favorite. Today we get chicken noodle soup and an egg salad sandwich.

Right after everyone is served, the show begins. Mr. and Mrs. Schmaltz, who have lost their connection with reality several years ago, are usually the center ring in this circus. That first lunch was a classic. Missus raised her hand into the air, stated quiet clearly, “Kasisichaistan,” and went face down in the soup. The lunch room assistants all converged to help her and in doing so, took their attention off Mister, who immediately dropped his trousers to his knees and went to the counter where he was flashing the toaster. Screams from older ladies, not sure if joy or terror. The excitement is electric.

By noon, everyone has returned to their room and the sounds of Andy Griffith is once again floating on the air. Wheeling through the hallways, I am lucky enough to find three gents, still wrapped pretty tight and they are looking for a fourth at pinochle. Later, I spend time on physical conditioning, trying to stand on my leg and moving the fingers on my right hand. The leg is still very painful and I stop when it becomes too swollen. One of my card playing buddies shows me the closet where the crutches are kept. I work most of the next day on learning how to walk with them. It is difficult as my right hand is still bandaged and swollen. On Friday, I begin to plan the great escape.

Saturday is the big day. After breakfast, I gather my belongings when no one is watching. I put them all in a bag and sit on them in the wheelchair. My billfold and shoes make me uncomfortable and I'm sitting very high. I feel conspicuous, as I ride around, but no one ever really looks at the person in a wheel chair. They all shift their eyes as they walk past, no one want to see what age and disease does to people. I hit the front door right at noon when all hands are gathered in the lunch room to make sure the circus doesn't get too far out of control. Once I make it outside the front door, I notice there is a slight downhill to the left, so I turn into it and let gravity help the wheelchair for the first block. I let it roll as far as possible then work to gain additional distance. Two blocks away, I change into my civilian clothes, nodding good morning to several ladies walking by. They have been watching me change from nursing home blues into civilian shorts and have a polite snicker when they see my skivvies. They return my greeting. I leave my institutional crap on the nursing home chair. Switch to the crutches and walk toward what I hope is downtown, with a smile on my face, freedom at last.

Fortunately a taxi comes by and gives me a ride. I have him take me to the Police Department, Joy, Joy, there is my Jeep. I go in and talk to the front desk Sergeant, who when he sees my driver's license, and the letter from Chuck, tosses me the keys. I stash my gear in the back, search throughout the vehicle for the pistol. It's is gone. I suspect Bob took it. That rat. I will have to notify Chuck to report it as stolen.

It turns out to be significantly more difficult to drive than I had imagined. There is no way I can get in from the driver's side. I find that I have to put my weight on my right leg to get in and there is just too much pain. I try sitting first and swinging my legs in, but there is not enough room.

Finally, I try the passenger's side, sit on the seat and slide in slowly, using the hand grip on the roll bar, and my left leg. I need to lean forward to get my posterior over the center console and then pull heavily on the steering wheel. Fortunately the Jeep console only extends several inches out onto the seat. Finally I do get over it. Now I use my arms to manually raise my left leg and lift it over the hump and down on the driver's side. My right leg is still hanging over the console and is painful, but at least I am in and can drive. I leave my right leg hang over on the passenger's side and drive with only my left leg. I spend a long time trying to find the dog shelter, but finally, I roll down the windows and drive toward the distant uproar of barking dogs.

Trying to get out of the Jeep is another exercise in pain and frustration. Without the hand grip that is slung down from the roll-bar, I probably would not have made it. It's still a slow and painful process. My right leg comes over the console with a thump, causing me more pain than I want to experience again. Eventually, I stand up on my crutches and work my way inside to see if they have my dog. Hooray, they bring him out. He still remembers me and showers my face with kisses. He either is beginning to like me or he hates the pound. Never can tell with the canine mind. I pay $129 of my last $150 to the shelter. Need to find an ATM soon.

A nervous, fearful, dog does not react well at all to crutches. It's difficult for both of us with him pulling on the leash, trying to keep his distance from those frightening stick things I'm carrying, while I try to maintain my balance on crutches. Quickly, he does his business and rushes for the back seat of the car. I go through the long struggle to get into the car again and he waits patiently in the back seat. Good dog. Thanks be to God he doesn't jump over the seat onto my leg. It was noon when I left the nursing home and by two o'clock I am watching Kill Devil Hill disappear in the rear view mirror.

Finally on my way to Florida, I suspect the crew in the nursing home is searching in the closets and bathroom for me. I probably owe them a lot of money, but the insurance and Medicare will handle most of it and I will contact them again when I reach Florida. I really wanted to invite Delightful Brunette with me, but I worried that she would turn me in. Besides, if she had offered to come with me, I might not have survived through the first night with that body of hers. And of course, there is that problem with the husband.

A misty rain begins to fall as I begin my drive to the south. My luck in attracting rain is continuing. I find an ATM at a drive through bank in Nags Head. I pull into the next big gas station as I'm down to a quarter of a tank. I roll down my window and shout at the guy next to me, "Could you give me a little help here?" He looks at me all hunched up over the center console and starts pumping gas for me. I give him the money and an extra ten bones. While I'm thanking him, he tells me, "You're in no condition to drive. It's people like you who cause most of the accidents. Glad I'm heading north away from you." Hooray for Good Samaritans anyway, even if they are too mouthy.

Dinner is purchased at a burger joint. Two quarter pounders, fries, and large water for the Bog. I pull off at next motel and begin the long process of getting out. The motel is accepting about having the dog and lets me stay with a modest deposit. I get a ground floor room, give Bogie his sandwich, walk him, then return to the room to rest. He curls up on the foot of the bed and goes out like a light. By the time I finish my food, I also am sleepy. This rest was so nice, I stay an additional day. Feeling much better, rested and the pain from my leg has begun to lessen, I strike out for sunny southern South Florida.

I leave in the early dark after a breakfast sandwich and coffee. Always best to feed Bogie before we leave so he can take care of business. A fast moving cold snap has turned the morning mist to light flurries and there are patches of dark ice on the highway. I hunch up over the steering wheel, trying to lessen the pain in my leg, listening to the radio on high, and hugging the inside of the lane. I am hoping more traffic will help melt the ice. If nothing else, riding the center, I will have more time to catch it if the car starts to slide. I drive along dreaming about the damage I am going to inflict on Bob and Arnie, which ever I find first. With all the trouble and pain caused by those two, damned if they don't both need a goodly amount of pain.

I have recovered enough by now to enter through the driver's side but I'm still only driving with my left leg. Walking and feeding the dog is getting easier. I should just get rid of this ugly little mutt of a dog with the long ears and rat-like tail but my wife's ghost would come back to get me. And perhaps, I am getting a little fond of him.

Bogie always seems excited when we take off. He jumps onto the dashboard with his front paws to watch the world sailing rapidly past him. He even barks a few times before he curls up and goes to sleep., Somehow having him here makes me feel the weight of my life sit less heavily on me. Perhaps in the future I can be a better man. But right now, I have to do something about Arnie after his merciless attack on me. But, looking at the little guy, and feeling my responsibility, I'm not sure that I'm what I'm planning is justice. It may be just part of my selfish vindictive nature. My decision will sit heavy until I can find Arnie.

Dirty snow collects slowly at the edges of the road. My trip has been extended significantly by being on the outer banks of North Carolina. The trip back is long and tedious on two-lane roads. It's still dark out and I spend a lot of time trying to read maps with tiny lettering. Weather, the crush of housing, and the continual bombardment of bill boards along the road, detracts from the beauty of the area. Now pain, dark ice, and misty snow, all combine to slow travel. I need another break. By eight that evening, I have purchased a large pizza, twelve pack of beer, fifth of bourbon, rented a motel room and have walked the dog. He's a smart little shit and now walks gently next to me. He seriously dislikes other men, making me believe that at some time he has been mistreated by one. I give him a piece of pizza on the rug by the door, a bowl of water, crawl into bed. Snort of Jack, sip of beer, bite of pizza, repeat. Twenty minutes later, I'm whacked and full. Soon I am asleep. Bogie is busy doing battle with the pizza I had left out.

Pick up mess in a.m.; wrap my leg with plastic bag supposed to be used for dry cleaning. Time for my first shower. The hot water just washes over me easing muscular aches. I have my right leg outside of the curtain so it should be okay. I have unwrapped my hand and am washing it. When I am done with the shower, I use a razor blade to cut the sutures and then remove them. My hand looks pretty good. Two fingers are still numb but they may still recover the feeling. I'm regretting drinking quite that much Jack the night before and decide that another day of rest will not be a bad idea.

It's one in the afternoon. Lying on the bed, just relaxing, I'm still reliving the events of the last three weeks. My back is quite painful from driving hunched over the steering wheel and doing all my driving with my now very swollen left leg. I need to rest and heal before the coming battle with Arnie. I call a friend, a true friend. Top Sergeant Larry Belton I served with him in the Corps. He is currently living in Port Saint Lucie, Florida, at a gated reserve called Breezy Palms. I think/hope he will put me up for a few weeks if I need it.

CHAPTER FIFTEEN
TOP BELTON

I call him early the next morning. It's still dark outside but his military training will never let him relax enough to let him stay in bed until the sun comes up. "Hey you sun-burnt, son of a sea jackal, how the fuck you doing?"

"Hey, that you, Doc?"

"Certainly, Top. I'm heading south, need a place to crash, thought I would pull in and set up camp at your place. You going to be home?"

"Of course, I'll be here. I'll just go ahead and kick some of these Miami Dolphin Cheerleaders out to make room for you. How long till you're here? Don't want to kick them out till I have to."

"About three or four days. Don't worry about the cheerleaders, you know they are all wild about me and I could use something soft to sleep on."

"How long can you stay?"

"I'm a little banged up, need time to heal up a little. I would like to stay at least a couple of weeks if you can bear putting in enough scotch to keep me that long."

"No prob, Doc.," he says. "See you when you get here. Gotta run now, trying to chase Bambi down."

First Sergeant Larry Belton had been the standard issue Marine asshole when I went to I-Corp in Vietnam on my first tour. He was loud and abrasive, apparently having little time to spend being friendly with a new Corpsman. He always waited to see if the new guys would stick and not wimp out. Somewhere along the time line during my first six months he must have decided that I was worth helping. I knew what a treasure he was. He was known as Top. The highest ranked non-commissioned officer in the company and therefore the most trusted. Officers always had their heads lost in regulations and planning and such crap as that. The non-coms translated what the officers told them into something that was both survivable and doable. I soon noticed the company could call Larry anything they wanted as long as they said it with respect and were friendly. Well, anything but Larry.

During my first major fire-fight with bullets zipping inches over my head, everyone hugging the ground tighter than they would have hugged Raquel Welch. I felt someone kick my foot. It was Top Belton.

"Doc, get up, we got work to do. Come on, get up, we got shit to do. Besides, you take up just as much room on the ground there as you would standing. If that gook bullet is going to get you, it will get you laying down or standing up. It's better standing up. You know these guys ain't Marine marksmen, they are Vietnamese, the worst shooters in the world. Try to get them to shoot at you and you are safer. They never hit anything except by accident."

His logic sucked, his courage was inspiring, I went with him. I never forgot the lesson. Safety is great but first you have to do your duty. When the lives in the balance are your responsibility, you worry about their lives first. And it worked. The better care I took of my Marines, the better care they took of me.

He had not been seriously wounded in combat. He had a couple of Purple Hearts but from minor wounds. The real damage came from the country we were in and the poison our country was pouring out on the ground from high flying aircraft. Agent Orange poison was rapidly draining the life out of him. He'd gone through two cancer surgeries already and now peripheral neuropathy was draining the sensation out of his legs and arms. It should be named 'slow creeping relentless death'. His body was failing him; he used a cane and a brace for his left leg to stop foot-drop. His personality was still half-alligator and half- alley cat. It would be good to see him and I want to see how Bogie likes Bambi, his pet cat.

CHAPTER SIXTEEN
MATT

I know it will be a long day. Bogie at my feet gives me his patented look of complete happiness. He has eaten and walked. Everything else, he simply could care less. Unlike me, he is happy, always lost in the moment. While I have to drive and do the worrying, gas, money, travel, all my bailiwick, nothing to him. Only thing seems to bother him is if I wear a cap, that scares him (someone with a cap on must have been mean to him).

It's taken me a full day to get from Nags Head out to Rocky Mount, where I am now. Right next to I-95. The east coast boulevard. Crank up the Jeep and we are headed south. Probably three days to Port Saint Lucie. It would be pleasant to stop at the large RV/Tent parks in Myrtle Beach. Everything good is available there. There is a community that gathers every winter-good music-good food-good company. It would be a relaxing time for Bogie and me. Maybe even 'Mrs. Calabash's' for some of that great seafood. But it's only a siren song, a mystic mermaid calling me. There is a fiend I must find. Retribution is a must for me. I cannot allow him to roam free after he tried to kill me. No looking over my shoulder, he is a dead-man walking. A sad tear comes to my eye as I pass the Florence turn-off to Myrtle Beach, but the Jeep keeps rolling south. I could have done justice to a plate of coconut shrimp.

My instincts tell me that Arnie is headed to Key West. He will easily merge into the tolerant life style of the Keys. Arts, Music, and Theater, all blossom into radiant colors up and down Duval Street. He will attempt to blend right in, but I will unblend him and then bury him. I also know that he is such a ham-bone that he might have thought he was good enough for New York.

Driving steady, I make it most of the way through Georgia that day. I am getting much better at in and out of the Jeep. I can exit much faster, then leash up Bogie and walk him. He is fast at the business end of a walk. A couple of cheeseburgers and we make it through to the evening. I stop just after dark and spend another night in deep sleep. I decide to spend another day here and go to big mart where they sell canes. I cover at least a mile on the cane that day. My leg swells up until it looks like a rhinoceros leg, but by morning it is pretty well back to normal. I left the crutches in the motel and headed out early.

By hitting it a little faster than legal, I manage to see the first exit to Port Saint Lucie by two that afternoon. Following Top's directions, I turn toward the ocean on St. Lucie Boulevard and hit it straight to US 1. Then south.

I drive down US 1 much slower than is acceptable by the resident population judging by the honks and fingers, I am collecting. A few miles after turning south, I see the turn to Breezy Pines. The entrance is announced on a large brick wall flanking the entry way. The first half block is lined with the advertised palm trees blowing in the breeze. With the turn off onto the narrow asphalt streets, everything looks to be large evergreen oaks or Norfolk Isle Pine trees. The park is comprised of short lots built to hold smaller mobile homes and is planted heavily with hedges and bushes. To me, it looks as if the park was established back in the sixties when ten foot by sixty foot mobile homes were the norm.

I start honking my horn half a block from where I think his place will be. Love to make an entrance and not only is Larry standing out front to see 'what the hell is going on,' several neighbors of his are also. Larry is up on the porch waving. Bambi is sitting on the wicker love seat by the front door. I get out slowly, while he waits, then shake hands, then give him a big hug. In the process, I whack him with the cane.

He looks the same to me after all these years. Bristly and tough as a pine cone from one of these loblolly pines.

"Damn, Top, you never going to change are you?"

He hands me a beer and invites me in. "Just a second," I tell him, "I brought a friend." I open the door to the Jeep and Bogie comes at a run. He stops at the top of the stairs looking at Bambi. He knows cats are supposed to run, but this one just looks at him. When Larry and I go in, he runs in also. There is a lot of snarling – hissing – hair standing on end. A few things get knocked over, not many broke, and by the time we finish our first beer, they have sorted out their territory. No serious blood.

Larry has put me into the first bedroom down the hall, he stays in the master bedroom all the way at the back of his home. It's not really a mobile home in anything but name, it's staked into the ground and has been for forty years. This area has hurricanes and every dwelling has to pass the strict safety codes. It's also connected to electricity and plumbed. Planted solid and never meant to be move, they transfer from one owner to another, but the land itself is owned by the Breezy Palms Company and the house owners pay rent for the land every month. My bedroom is eight feet by ten feet, with a small closet for clothing. I have a single bed and also put down a small bed for Bogie. He, being a strange little dude, never uses it, he always crawls under the bed to sleep. He can barely squeeze through the tiny space, but I can hear him working his way to the back by the wall. He must feel he needs security from that beast of a cat.

I wake early that first morning and walk out to the front of Top's house to get the paper. It is a cool quiet morning. It has rained during the night and the freshness of the air is invigorating. Looking at the papers and not paying too close attention to my surroundings, I am surprised when a large bobcat breaks cover from the hedge next to me and tears off for the river. Lord, what a beautiful place.

"Larry, you live in paradise. I been thinking if any place is open for sale when I finish killing these sad bastards, I will come back here to live."

"Not to fear, Doc, This park is age fifty five restricted. Many of the original owners have been here since in opened in 1982. Someone's always dying off here. We will get you a place."

After breakfast and a second cup of coffee, I walk over to Collector Comics to see Keith. He is only three blocks from Top's place. I have been a little worried about how he is doing with Harry. He is just opening up as I walk up. We say a quick hello, shake hands and hug, then stand to one side and let the waiting customers in. Keith is all business man. His customers come first, always. I try to talk but everyone has a question and he is busy running to find the specific comic that they were unable to locate. He tells me that Harry did not work out. "Had to get rid of him.

We just didn’t click. Talk about it at lunch okay. I'll call you when Jerry gets in. Love ya, great to have you back.” And he runs off to help another customer.

I walk back to Top's. Time to check in with Frank. He's glad I made it down okay, but no action going on that looks like our guy. This seems most strange, up north the action was fast, down here nothing. I'm thinking he's getting smarter and hiding the bodies. Finding him may be more difficult than I thought. I still think Arnie went all the way down to Key West.

CHAPTER SEVENTEEN
KEITH

I am eating lunch with Keith at The Cottage, a busy restaurant just down from Collector Comics. Tough part about eating at a great restaurant in a small building is the noise and bustle. Still the waitress staff is great, food excellent, and they make the best burgers around. I order another masterpiece taking full advantage of the cook, Cajun spice, jalapeños, blue cheese, medium rare with all the garden stuff thrown in. Keith orders his medium rare, with nothing but bun and fries. Many years ago I stopped trying to reform his dietary habits and improve his life. I also order a half liter of Mondavi Cabernet Sauvignon, while he orders a diet Pepsi. I think the earthiness of the wine adds significantly to the flavor of the beef but there is no way I would ever convince Keith to try it. He tried red wine once and didn't like it.

He looks much the same as when I last saw him three years ago. A scraggly semi-beard on his face from not shaving for the last two weeks, a ratty superhero tee and jeans. He's a good twenty pounds overweight now and cares not at all. The clothes and the weight do not hide the strength he has from his years as a Hollywood stunt man.

I met Keith about ten years ago through his father, a World War II Vet, who was tough and funny. He was a master at getting things over on Keith, and he would laugh about it for days. Even now, I am maintaining the tradition and will stick Keith with the bill anytime I can get it over on him. Planned it long before I came. I suspect his dad is somewhere chuckling.

How well you like this new Jerry?"

"Pretty good guy. I plan on making him an assistant, if he learns enough to answer some of the questions. Soon I will do nothing but manage."

"What happened with Harry?"

"That's a strange story. He started out great. Worked hard, learned fast. Then about the fourth day, Dave of Mad Dog Comix called me. Said he had bought a Hulk number 181 for only six hundred from a tall guy he hadn't seen before. He recognized the comic as one I had on my wall only three weeks ago. Thought I ought to know. When I approached Harry about it, he gave me that 'Not me' routine. It wasn't what he said though; he said it like of course I took it, what you going to do about it. I told him to take a hike. He's a different type of guy, Matt. He seemed to get what he wanted, then he didn't want it anymore because he had it. The other thing is that he didn't know is most of us comic people support all the other comic people. Dave brought my comic back couple days ago."

"Sorry I called about him. He appeared to be so sincere about having a good job."

"Big difference between seem and be. You couldn't know. He is one weird fuck."

Keith takes about five bites out of his burger and he still has three fourths of it left. For a guy with a big mouth, who talks all the time, he takes tiny bites. "This is how burgers are supposed to be, not with all that goat food on 'em." When the waitress walks by, he stops her for another Pepsi and more fries. I put in an order for onion rings, just to jack up the bill a little.

"It's good to be back in town," I bite into mine. I have it stacked too high and it's messy but beautiful. Take a little drink of wine. "I'm actually thinking of moving back and staying put. This homeless bit with the open road and adventure around every curve is starting to get old. Plus, I found a little place I can afford."

"I gotta see it to believe it. Money wasn't the reason you hit the road, you knew you could always have moved in with Monica and me. You did the road cause you like the road. Don't think you ever had enough common sense just to sit back and enjoy. And what about the guy from the Appalachian Trail you are trying to find? Top told me you are on another crusade trying to right another wrong. Matt, the Eagle Scout, going to just sit back and take it easy. I gotta see it."

"Did I mention to you that my cow died?'

"No, when did you get a cow?"

"Just letting you know I don't need your bull."

"That is one pitiful joke. Pitiful."

"Yeah, I hear you. The thing is, I just don't know where to look for him anymore. I can't do much till I hear of him in action again. Now the little bastard that hit me with the car, I am still planning on going down to Key West and kill him. My leg still hurts. Whatcha doing tomorrow, take a road trip with me. We can find and drown that little twerp, drag him out in the ocean and wax his sorry ass, then I'll buy you a sloppy joe from Sloppy Joe's. Tell me that doesn't sound good."

"It sounded good till you said that crap about a sloppy joe. Don't they have burgers down there? Anyway, me and Monica have a gig tomorrow. Why don't we grab the poles and go fishing? Besides, we can get him anytime. Let him relax a little and drop his guard. Revenge served cold and all that."

"Come to think of it, got to take my little guy to the Vet. Just need to get him checked out. Hey, let me get the check for this. Oh, wait, I forgot my billfold, damn, could you pick it up this time and I get it next time?"

"You jerk, you don't think I know how long you planned this, and I walk right into it? No problem, I'll get it, but you gotta get the next one. Swing by tomorrow and we'll talk."

CHAPTER EIGHTEEN
ARNIE AND HARRY

The disappointment is intense after the trip south. Keith and Matt had promised him the job, then Keith canned him just on suspicion of stealing a comic after he had already told Lorraine he had the job. He really needed that six hundred to get set up, it wasn't like he was a thief. Now he and Arnie were camping on the beach north of town, near the nuclear plant. They move several times a week to avoid the police.

The money has been extremely tight until the last victim. He sounded like he was speaking German and he had over fifteen hundred in his wallet. Thank God for tourists that like to walk on beaches. He is using the quick kill agenda trying to avoid detection. He has killed four now since coming here. They bury the victims in the sand a few yards off the beach near the power plant. Few fishermen go out there because the nuclear plant heats the water and fish avoid the area.

They are both ready to leave, but feel they owe Matt and Keith. Pain for pain. Kill them both, then they can leave.

Arnie found out where Matt is staying this afternoon. He was in the arcade, playing Space Invaders, watching the Cottage, until Matt and Keith had gone in to eat. In his wig and beach hat, Matt had not noticed Arnie while he tailed him back to the mobile home. Harry would be elated. Maybe now they could get moving again. It was just bad luck that Arnie hadn't killed Matt with the car. Stupid bad luck.

CHAPTER NINETEEN
MATT

That evening, Larry grills a fresh tilapia coated in a light lemon sauce. I make up a fresh spinach salad with onions and cucumbers. Sweet eats on a summer eve. After clean-up, we sit with cold beers watching the night fall. I have pretty well decided I will retire here after I cook Arnie's grits. It will be a wonderful way to spend the years I have left.

"It would be great to have you as a neighbor."

"I love it here. What could be better?" I lie awake for a long time making future plans, then revising them again and again. I know I have unfinished business with Arnie and the AT monster. When I hear of him being back in action again, I will go for him. Until then, I will wait here and take life easy. Still, for me it would be difficult to just settle in one place again, but I am determined to try.

Then, Bogie comes scurrying out from under the bed and goes into the living room, "What the hell is that all about," I mumble. He never comes out at night because he tries to avoid Larry and Bambi. Maybe there is food left out. I can't hear him eating. He's pacing back and forth from kitchen to living room. Claws clicking in kitchen, then quiet on living room carpet. I have to trust his senses. They are much sharper than mine. Something outside has alerted him. I slip out of bed to go check on him. Maybe he is sick and needs to go outside. I walk out to the living room in the dark and sit on the couch. He immediately jumps on my lap. He is tense and on full alert, looking and listening to something in the back yard.

There is someone outside in the yard. From the fear Bogie is exhibiting, it must be a man. Nothing else would affect the little guy like this.

"What is it little buddy?"

Ka-Boom – Ka-Boom – Ka-Boom. Someone, in the backyard, has fired a shotgun at the house. I can feel the floor shudder. A forty year old pre-made house is not that sturdy to start with. The mobile home has been hit three times and each hit has felt like a small earthquake tearing through the house. I rush to the window to see if I can see who is there. I hear Larry fire his Colt 45 at the rear of the house. Then there is silence. "We are under attack. Top, watch out they can shoot right through these walls."

"Saw two guys out there," says Larry. "They were scurrying away as fast as they could motor. They better fucking run, the sons a bitches put a hole in my house."

I can see nothing through the window. I open the front door slowly, still find nothing and step out into the cool dark. Nothing is moving. Then, I hear foot steps running north. Down the steps and out onto the road, walking as fast as I can, I realize this is hopeless. No shoes, no pants or shirt, back to the house before the police throw me in jail. I shout to Larry as I come closer, don't want to go down under friendly fire. He shouts back for me to come on in.

"You okay, Doc?"

"Sure, I'm not hurt."

"You got some bad people after you, Matt. Those shots tore the hell out of your bed. Damn, they wanted you dead, whoever they are."

"My bed? Why my bed? I don't know anyone down here. Maybe three or four people at the most. I thought they were all my friends."

"Well, you know it wasn't me. And I saw two men out there. You better start reconsidering who your friends are."

I put on the lights and got dressed. "Top, I'm heading out north to see if I can find these guys. I know they are probably gone, but I gotta look." I threw on my shorts, shoes, and grabbed my K-Bar. "Who in the hell even knew where I was staying?"

I run out into the night. I can hear the traffic two blocks over on US 1. Nothing else. I begin to walk slowly, senses on high alert. They still have to be out here somewhere. Top said he had seen two figures. I have at least that many enemies out to kill me, maybe more. Very slowly I walk around the perimeter of the park but see nothing moving.

This time, I go over to US 1 and walk up the sidewalk heading south. Again I walk slowly, listening, and watching for anything.

Since I have not heard a car start or drive away, I am assuming whoever it was is on foot and carrying a shotgun. That should be noticeable.

As I go by the strip mall with the comic store in it, I hear a noise from behind the mall. Someone is fighting. I can hear Keith's voice and I walk as fast as I can. He's fighting with Harry and Arnie in the dark behind the store. As soon as I see Arnie, it becomes clear to me that it has been Harry and Arnie the whole time. How could I have been so stupid? I just didn't tie Arnie into a partnership with Harry.

Keith is guarding one arm while trying to wrestle Harry off with the other. Arnie is trying to wrap a rope around Keith's legs. I shout loudly to get Arnie's attention, then draw my knife and walk directly at Arnie, waving the knife in a figure eight motion at his face. He immediately backs off dropping the rope and starts going for the car. I follow him. He is reaching for a shotgun, which I knock from his hands with a hard swing of the knife and kick the gun under the car. Arnie gives up the idea of the shotgun and runs into the comic store. I return to help Keith with Harry. Harry's back is turned to me and I am able to cut him on his right upper arm. Then strike viciously at his neck. Harry sees my blow coming and dodges the strike. He stops fighting with Keith and runs after Arnie into the comic store.

Once there is room between us, I can see that Keith's left arm is bent at a funny angle several inches above his wrist. But he still leads the charge into the store, so I know I have some help. A box of books comes sailing through the air and hits Keith's shoulder, but he muscles his way through the onslaught and heads for his desk. I go right through the office area into the main body of the store and see that Arnie is pulling the valuable comics off the wall while Harry is busy throwing boxes of comics and toys at us. Smoke is filling the store; Arnie has taken all the valuable books off the wall and is now building a fire from other comics. Arnie gets the front door open and runs out into the street with Harry right behind him.

I stop at the door and watch as they head across the highway and disappear into the tangle of brush. If I follow the two of them, they will kill me.

Keith comes out of the office with a fire extinguisher and pretty well stops the flames. The pile of semi-burned comics is smoldering. I push them out the front door with a broom. Keith tells me, "I have called the police. They should be here in a minute. Damn, Matt, it was good to see you come around the corner there. I'm sure I would have subdued them both anyway, but your help made it faster."

"Oh yeah. You were up to your ass in alligators. Don't think they were both just about to surrender to your sorry ass."

"Matt, you don't think I had them on the run?" He chuckled. "Damn good thing you came, but I will never admit to it again."

"Grab us a soda out of that cooler, will you?" Keith says. He opens the bottom drawer in his desk and pulls out a bottle of rum. "Want a hit?"

I light one of my cigars, take the bottle of rum, and to his protests about smoking in his store, I take a deep pull. "Nothing better." Then I go outside to finish my cigar in peace. Keith has always been a health nut and gives me tons of grief about the cigars. Well, what can you do with a Captain America fan?

Keith had been working late at the store when he heard the door handle turn on the back door. He had left it unlocked because Monica was coming to join him. He wasn't worried until he saw it was Harry. Keith had immediately gone for his gun in the desk drawer, but Harry had hit him with a staff before Keith could get to it. His left arm was injured and he backed away from Harry to protect it. Harry was too fast. He grabbed Keith and the two of them began to wrestle in the corner of his office. Keith struggled to get free and protect his injured left arm at the same time. Arnie had joined the fray. He was trying to tie a rope to Keith's legs. The other end is still attached to the car. They were going to drag him. Then I had entered the fight and evened up the sides.

The Police and Fire Department arrive at the same time. While one officer takes statements from Keith, me, and Top Belton who had arrived by that time. The three remaining officers go in pursuit of Harry and Arnie.

The Fire Department did a wonderful job, the fire had been extinguished but they had soaked everything down to prevent a flame up later. Everything in the store was a total loss. Smoke, fire, and water damage ruined everything. Everything was closed up, Keith went to the Hospital and Top and me went back to

Breezy Palms to sleep. Just another day of excitement in Port Saint Lucie, Florida.

The next morning, I called Frank. Arnie and Harry have been busy. There were at least four bodies discovered buried in shallow graves near the Power Plant. The two have escaped capture and are now officially at points unknown. Frank tells me that all members of the state and local police in Florida have been put on alert in an attempt to capture these two.

I take a cup of coffee, a cigar, and I walk down to the river. Sit on the bank, light the cigar, sip my coffee, and watch the water flow past. I just finish the coffee and half of the cigar when Top comes down to join me with the pot of coffee to refill my cup.

"How you doing, Matt?"

"Doing good, Top. I got it. I know where they went. Going to have to leave tomorrow for awhile. Maybe a couple of months. Will you watch Bogie for me?'

"Sure, he's no prob. Where do you think they went?"

"I'm sure they went back to the Trail. I think they went right to the Southern entry place in Georgia, and now are moving north. It's the only place Harry feels safe."

"Kinda a long shot, ain't it?"

"Nope. I'm certain. I'll go tomorrow morning, be back in six weeks or less with their scalps."

CHAPTER TWENTY
MATT

I have been on the Trail for ten days now. I am not hiking or traveling at all. I set up my camp thirty yards off the traveled sectors, where I can see the Trail and hikers, while remaining unseen myself. Realizing that if someone is going slow and searching for me, they will be able to find me, I still do my best at camouflaging my tent. It's set up down off the trail, I have covered it with branches and leaves making it difficult to detect from a distance of more than twenty feet. It also makes it a haven for nasty biting little insects that are resistant to the cold. I have a thick layer of insect repellent covering all exposed parts of my body. From where I am camped, I can climb straight up the side of the mountain and with the help of a small, stout tree am able to work my way up to the top of a large granite boulder, whose sides have been worn smooth by long years exposed to the elements. There I can lay motionless and watch the trail while remaining unseen myself. This would seem to be the perfect strategy to find them if in fact they are using the trail. So far, everything in me says this is where they will now go for safety. Hopefully I will be able to see them coming. Then I can follow and devise some way to take them down.

Nothing ever seems to work as planned. It is mid-morning, I crawl down from the boulder to get rid of morning coffee, walk around the boulder to stretch my legs, and there stands Arnie, watching me. He is on the Trail; I am ten yards away, down the mountainside, probably fifteen feet below him. The Trail itself is hard packed dirt here, it has five large trees along the far edge, but this edge is free of growth. Down below me, the mountainside is green with trees and undergrowth. It's still only about ten in the morning and it's beautiful today at sixty five degrees.

"Nice to see you again, Matt."

"Hey Arnie, what a surprise to see you here," I answer.

"I don't think it's much of a surprise," he responds in a singsong voice. “I had so hoped to be through with you. I told Harry I thought we lost you in Port Saint Lucie, but you do tend to hang on a man's trail like grim death. How did you ever manage to find us?”

“Actually, it was pretty easy. The Trail is Harry's security blanket. He feels better here than anywhere else in the world. He also feels impervious to harm. Since you two are much faster hikers than me, I had to jump ahead to catch up. I traveled straight to Great Smokey Mountain Park and hiked up from there. So I only had to hike ten miles to get here. I figured you two would have taken a bus to Americola, Ga. It's the cheapest way to travel and the closest entry point to the Trail. Plus, I think for you, the best way to avoid the police.

“You know us too well, Matt. I am going to have to kill you, just to be rid of you.”

“Every crow in the forest thinks he is the blackest, Arnie, and you are just letting your mouth run now. That little ass of yours would have a hard time messing with me. I got no worries until Harry gets here. By then I will be gone and moving on.”

“You old douche. I can beat the crap out of you without breathing hard. Once I subdue and tape you up, we'll wait for Harry. He will do great things with you. He was up most of the night with an older schoolteacher who wandered into our camp last night. I'm surprised you didn't hear the screams up here. He was a tough old goat and fought death longer that I would have believed. I don't suppose it's really funny, but it was funny if you were there, cause one of his eyes just flopped out and laid on his cheek, kinda looking at the ground, and then at the same time the other eye explodes. Throws juicy crap all over camp. He's already dead then, of course. Anyway, Harry has learned to hide the site of the fire better now, but it takes time. That's what he's doing now with that little shovel he bought.

“Aw Arnie, that isn't you at all. You're sensitive and a thespian. How in the hell did you get wrapped up with that crazy bastard. Why don't you come with me and get away from Harry altogether. You know you will be happier and live longer.”

“I love Harry. I'm staying with him.”

“You can always fall in love again, Arnie. I mean, if you don't want to go back with Bob, there will still be someone that deserves your love. Someone to cherish you the way you deserve to be cherished. Something else you really should be thinking about. Although, I suspect you know it by now since you are hiking a ways in front of Harry. One day soon, when the blood lust is on him, he will want to extend his time of power and keep his sacrifice alive much longer. You will be main item on his menu. He will take a long, long time with you.

"Harry loves me."

"I think he does too. That's why he's so dangerous. What he inflicts on you will be through love. It will only add a more delicious spice to his fire. He is one sick puppy, but then, I don't suppose you're wrapped all that tightly yourself."

"Arnie, why don't you consider giving yourself up to me? I will take you down to the local police. It will take years to get everything sorted out and the only thing I know we can prove right now is that you were involved with a hit and run. That was in North Carolina, you know, Florida doesn't extradite to other states. Plus, they will put you in with the general population and that may well turn out to be the best years of wild sex you ever have. Lots of big bad guys in there looking for a cutie like you. I'm sure they will love you as much as Harry does."

"It's tempting, Matt, but I don't think so. I think this might be the perfect time to give a great present to Harry and get you off our trail at the same time. We think you may be hoarding piles of money in that back pack of yours. It be enough to keep us living high for several months. Harry will have so much fun cooking you up that he won't think about me for months."

He starts to come off the Trail and down the incline toward me. I am below him on the mountain and it is steep enough that I am unsteady on my feet. I don't have any good lateral movement anyway because of my left knee. There is no flee option here, fight or die, is all I get to choose from. When Arnie is still about eight yards above me, I throw a baseball size rock at him. I lean into it, putting weight and speed behind it. It hits him mid-body and knocks him backwards a little, he grunts heavily, but rights himself and continues to come at me. I rapidly throw a second rock but hurry my throw and he blocks it with his left arm. Now at only two yards away, I pull my knife and slash at his left leg which is closest to me. I miss his leg, but have my knife close to my body and stab forward toward his body, the biggest target, with what strength I can muster. I hope to hit him where the knife can cut into his intestines and do the most good, but my thrust goes in off to the right side of his abdomen, more into the muscle between the hip bones and the ribs. He cries aloud with pain and crashes into me on his rush down the mountain. I try to dodge him to the right, but his arm catches me and the force of his jump and gravity works to pull me over backward. I have lost the grip on my knife and it remains embedded in his abdomen. With him hanging on to me, the two of us go flying down the side of the mountain. We are rolling together trying to land blows as we go. He is much stronger than I thought he would be. He is hurting me with his fists, my nose is bleeding and I think he may have broken a rib. He rolls into a curled up position, trying to protect further damage to his stomach. I reach for him and pull him close, just as we smash into a fair sized tree. Hitting mid-body, both of us take a powerful body blow. It stuns me for several seconds. We are laying side by side, my arm is too close to his mouth and he bends his head forward and bites a chunk of flesh off my the right shoulder. It is painful and unexpected. I literally jump my body off the ground about six inches and come down pretty much on top of him. He is still swinging his arms trying to hit me, but the bulk of my body keeps him from getting enough leverage into his arms to hurt me. His face is level with mine. The arch of the forehead can be an incredibly strong and useful weapon. I pull my head back and head butt him as hard as I can in the middle of his face. I feel his teeth cut the skin above my eyes, but I also feel his nose break. Pulling my head back again, I look at him, I know he is defeated. His face is a mess. He is having a difficult time breathing with the damage to his face and my weight laying on him. I have him now, I just need to wait. He can't really injury me in any way. The blood loss from his knife wound and the difficulty in breathing are rapidly draining his will to resist. Finally, he lays still, trying to catch his breath through the blood and mucus pouring down his throat.

I am stuck in a moderate dilemma. He is so much faster than me that if I am interpreting his exhaustion incorrectly, and let him up too soon, he will have me. But if I wait much longer he will be dead. I finally conclude that the cumulative damage I have inflicted has him almost unconscious. I roll off him slowly and start to stand, forcing myself up on my feet with my hands and arms. He is lying still. I see that the knife in his abdomen has seriously wounded him. During the fight, the blade has moved several inches, probably perforating his lower intestine. I give him a hand to help him stand up and together we struggle up the mountain and onto the trail. He lies down immediately. I tape his hands together, just in case. Then pull his trousers down to reveal the wound.

"Arnie, this is bad. If I pull out the knife, it will start a massive internal bleeding and you will be dead soon after that. I am going to tape around it to hold it in place and stop the bleeding. We'll let the doctors' deal with it. I am unable to get any cell signal here, so I am going to walk back to where I can call in help for you. I may have to return to town but I will go as far as I need to get you some help. As soon as possible I will have a rescue crew coming to help you. I slap duct tape across the wound and around the knife. I try to clean his face enough to help him breath easier.

"Wounded as you are, I would caution you to be quiet. If Harry finds you, he will play his bad games with you. I wish you had agreed to be my prisoner, together, we might have gotten you down to the village before Harry caught us. I'm really sorry it came to this, Arnie."

He motions me to come closer, "Fuck you Matt. Hope he gets you soon."

Sitting him up against a tree, I take my back pack, my staff and set off down the Trail to get help. I have left my tent and most gear. Hopefully it will be okay. I have it pretty well hidden, and Harry may not suspect that I left it behind.

I make it to the turn off from the Trail down to the Smokey Mountain Camp Grounds and begin the long slow hike down. My left knee, with the prosthesis, is swollen and painful. That roll down the mountain has not helped it. It doesn't bend very well at the best of times, and now is not the best of times. I move down the Trail slowly, careful, and take a long time in my descent. I truly don't think Arnie will make it anyway. With that perforated colon he will be lucky to live more than a couple of hours. He will be dead before the Rangers get here. If the abdominal wound doesn't kill him, Harry will. It probably would have been more merciful to just kill him and save him the agony but I just don't have it in me to execute a helpless human. But I don't mind him suffering and dying. I don't even try to make that rescue call on my cell phone.

At the Park Headquarters, I tell the Rangers that a hiker has fallen on his knife. That I have given him first aid to the best of my ability. I give his location. Mention absolutely nothing about a fight or who he is. Then hike out of the park, hitch a ride to a motel. Two blocks down the road is a drug store, I purchase dressings and iodine, cold cereal and milk, and return to the motel. A wonderful long hot shower, then I dress the wound on my arm where he bit me. The little bastard. Two quick bowls of cereal and into the bed. I am exhausted. Sleep, luscious, glorious sleep.

I stay in the motel for two days, eating three squares, sleeping until noon, healing up. On the third morning, I call Frank.

Arnie's body has been discovered. They believe he was killed by an assailant or assailants unknown. There has been no report of Harry or any action that would indicate the presence of Harry, other than the death of Arnie.

I will go back up tomorrow to find Harry. He will not leave the Trail. I eat a large breakfast, gather my gear, and head back up the mountain. I know Harry will be north of where I left Arnie. I will go north until I find some sign of him. I have a month left in the six week period I gave Top.

CHAPTER TWENTY-ONE
HARRY

"Hi Arnie." Harry is squatting next to Arnie looking at him.

"Harry, I was hoping you would come to help me. Matt stabbed me."

"I see." Harry moves Arnie's arms aside and pulls the knife out.

Arnie screams, the sight of his intestines starting to emerge terrifies him. The pain and the knowledge of what is coming is more than his mind can bear.

"I better go get some wood together," Harry says. "I don't want you getting cold tonight."

Arnie watches Harry go north on the Trail to find wood. He struggles against the tree he is leaning on. He manages to brace one hand, then holding his wound closed with the other hand, pushes his way to a standing position. He tries to walk but has little strength and the pain is intense. Still the fear of Harry pushes him on and he manages to stagger forty yards down the Trail before he is forced to hold on to another tree to catch his breath. If he can make it to where the Trail leads down to the Smokey Mountain Park, maybe he can pick up enough speed with the downward slope to stay ahead of Harry until he can get to where the small stream is. The stream will soothe him and carry him to the park. He begins to walk again with big strides but takes less than ten before he knows absolutely that he can go no farther. With nowhere to go, there can be only one escape to what is coming with Harry, he walks to the edge of the Trail and at a steep pitch on the mountainside, he throws himself over the edge, face first.

Harry carries the wood and follows the blood trail. There will be no problem finding his prey. He estimates that any rescue party coming must be at least a couple of hours away. As slowly as Matt was walking down the mountain, it will probably be much longer than that. He finds the slope that Arnie went over and works his way down. Poor Arnie has tried for a broken neck and death, but only has broken a leg in the fall. A little more pain in addition to what has already happened. It is not as if he isn't in bad shape anyway.

"Let me help you with that leg first," says Harry. He uses Matt's knife to cut the pants and shirt off Arnie. Then he unties the shoes, removes them and his socks. He lays several sticks next to the leg with strips of rope under the leg and sticks. He pulls Arnie's leg straight, then holds it with one hand while he ties it in place with the other. 'First leg, I've ever set and a pretty good job,' he thinks. Arnie's scream of pain is still echoing down the trail. Harry has enjoyed the pain Arnie exhibits when he pulled that leg to straighten it. The way it was swelling up, Arnie would have died rapidly if the leg had not been set Harry pulls his duct tape out and closes the wound on Arnie's abdomen. Then he walks off a few yards, lights a cigar, looks at his friend, lover, companion, and now play thing/victim. He begins to build a little fire. "This should be enough to keeps us warm, what do you think, Arnie?"

Arnie is at first been hopeful when Harry sets his leg. Now with the fire already started, he loses all hope. No longer does he answer Harry. He is lost deep inside himself, long dark passages filled with anguish and dead dreams stretch out mist-like before him. He longs for Bob to hold him in his arms one more time.

"This little piggy was the first to get cooked." Harry uses Matt's knife to cut the pinky off Arnie's his left foot and throws it on the fire.

"You never really needed these did you?" He cuts off Arnie's genitals and stuffs them in Arnie's mouth. "Figured you would want to know what your own tastes like before you die." A low moan is coming from the back of Arnie's throat.

Harry just sits and watches him spasm in pain as he works to continue breathing. He is loosing blood rapidly. He runs a strip of duct tape up Arnie's crotch in an attempt to stem the blood flow. Harry pushes some of the burning ashes onto Arnie's lap, that should cauterize the wound. Arnie's body writhes wildly for more than a minute, then his movements slow.

It takes a wonderfully long ten minutes for Arnie to pass. Harry watches in ecstasy. Dark greasy smoke fills the air. It has a sweet pork-like odor.

"Hate to see you go so soon Arnie, you were a good buddy and

I will miss you. I don't know if it will help, but I plan on spending a lot more time with Matt."

CHAPTER TWENTY-TWO
MATT

I am walking north for the third day. I have not seen Harry but I have seen signs that someone has been using the trails. I am at least fifteen miles north of where Arnie's body was discovered.

The trail here runs three feet wide, indicating to me that this part and its trails are used significantly more than the Appalachian Trail. Although the Smokey Mountain National Park trails tie into the Appalachian Trail system, they are different entities and maintained by separate groups. The trail drops off steeply near Copper Walnut Bottom Campsite where I am set up. Far below, I can see water running. The Smokey Mountains have an abundance of fresh running water.

The vegetation is thick beneath the canopy of trees. The time of year has erased much of the color, but significant beauty still remains. What I am happy about is that the snakes are all hibernating. The occasional bear is still out and roaming, but the idea of a rattler rubbing up against me during the night, bothers me more than the occasional black bear.

I am enjoying the majesty and beauty of the view until Harry rounds the bend of the trail and walks up close to me.

"Hi Matt," he says, "Imagine meeting you here."

"You knew I would come, Harry. I've seen sitting here trying to find a way out of this for you and me. It's a damn shame, but I can't see anyway out. I think that you and I are friends now and could have always been friends. The fact of the matter is, you cannot help who you are and I have to come after you."

"When did you figure out it was me?"

"I pretty well knew at Assateague Island. Had no proof, just suspicions, but there was something in the change of your personality the day after that fisherman was killed, that pointed to you. You were so mellow that day, I thought you were using marijuana, but I think killing is pretty much a drug for you."

"We still had a fine trip, didn't we? That fight with the gang was great."

"Yes. Shame in many ways," I say, shaking my head, "You are a good traveling companion, dependable and reliable. Wish I had known you before all this shit started."

"You wouldn't have liked me then, Matt. I didn't even like me back then. Strange thing, it is that which makes me unacceptable to society is that which makes my life bearable to me."

"Well, let's us sit and talk for a bit. No sense in being in a hurry. Not like we don't have months before anyone comes poking around here." I take my back pack and open it, rummage around a bit and pull out a pack of cigars. I light one, inhale deeply. Hold one out to him. "You want one?" While my hand is in the pack, I thumbed the top off the Vaseline petroleum jar. I scoop a huge dollop out into my palm.

Harry lights his cigar.

"Is there any chance you came here to give yourself up to me?" I ask. "You're younger and faster than me, Harry. You know I am not going to subdue you. Still in the long run, if you give up to me, it will save you a lot of trouble and pain. I will take you to the Sheriff and he will give you a nice warm room and three squares until they take you in on the gurney for a dirt nap. You'll be famous. Probably make a movie of you. All things considered, it's not that bad of a way to go. Plus, some knucklehead will probably write a book about you. You could die famous."

"No, I ain't thinking about giving up yet, Matt. It's just that I really don't want to hurt you. Even though, we both know I am going to. You know I don't want to kill you Matt, but how else do I get you to stop following me. Besides, you would turn me in to the authorities and they would hunt me down."

I have a smile on my face. My insides are gripped tight in fear. Everything in me urges me to run from him. I try to keep talking low and friendly.

"In a way you are lucky Matt, you will be dying in paradise." He turns to gesture to the wilderness around us.

"Harry, I've known you for better than a month now. You were always a solid citizen. What the hell happened to you?"

"I don't think I can even tell it exactly right or show you what it has meant, but I'm going to lay it on you as best I understand it myself. After that, I am just going to go on living it. I'm telling you, Matt, because it doesn't really matter. I'm going to kill you soon, so what I say will die with you. At least, I will have said it and maybe we both can understand it a little better after that."

I don't interrupt him. I wanted him to go on talking as long as possible while in my mind I am trying to find some way out of this.

"I was happy in my little life. I loved my wife, did my job conscientiously, paid my bills on time, kept my little bungalow up, and mowed my lawn. I went to work five days a week and spent the weekends catching up with family things and reading. Life was the same week in and week out. Sex every three days whether I wanted it or not. I had two weeks vacation every year and we spend it in Atlantic City, laying on the sand and watching the ocean. And Lorraine and I would look at each other and say, 'Isn't this wonderful.' That was it, that was my life.

"Everything changed with the shoe seller. His death was the catalyst. It was horrible and terrible and totally unnecessary. Easily the most satisfying thing I've ever done in my life.

"To me, he was a nothing with no real existence and when I took everything from him, my previous life was revealed to be the same mediocrity that his was. My existence had been built solid. And it was rock solid. But it was so tiny, my life was like a dollhouse in a closet. Every move in my previous life had been predicated on a false presumption of security, a security that sucked the very life from my bones. Social Security, savings for retirement, life insurance for my wife and future children, I had followed the rules all my life, school, work, college, all to get a non-descriptive life with no meaning. Do you really think I could go back to that?

"Now for the first time, I was free. I was walking across the Sahara sands, blindfolded, and I knew that at any second, a chasm could open before me and swallow me. I was alive – excited – terrified. My flopper was so big I needed a wheelbarrow to carry it. And then when I lit the fire and watched it from the park, knowing that the shoe seller was burning, there could be no return. My canoe was already shooting down stream out of control. I could see the waterfall ahead but there was no way to change it. If I had a paddle, I would have thrown it away. No more peanut butter and jelly sandwiches for me, now it is prime rib and caviar.

"You are going to tell me they will catch and kill me soon. I know that. While I am alive for only a short time, I am going to be fully alive every second of it."

"Well, Harry, I can tell you now that you won't return to a boring life again. You are not going to die sitting in a lawn chair watching a sunset. As your good buddy, I am going to make sure you go out exciting. Your days of libraries and soft tomorrows are gone."

As he turns away, I smear the Vaseline jelly on my wrists and forearms as thick as I can.

I have my staff in one hand. But so does Harry. He is taller, faster, and stronger than I am. This may be just a little rough to get out of. Not sure how loud I can shout, but there is no help for fifty miles and I doubt they would hear me.

"I know we will get it on soon, but there is no hurry, Harry, what say we have some hash and a cigar?" I reach back into my pack, feel a sharp pain on the side of my head, and down, down, down, I go. Blackness is there waiting for me.

My brain awakes with a scream. I come a long way down empty corridors. I remember that I am searching but am unsure what I search for. When full consciousness does return, I keep my eyes closed. I try to move but find I am unable to move arms or legs. They are bound and motionless. He has duct taped my arms from my hand to my elbows, forcing both arms together. He has taped my legs from my ankles up to my knees, force both legs together and it looks like he put at least two layers of tape on both my arms and legs. In addition, he has taped my wrists to my ankles so I am bent way out of shape. I haven't been able to touch my toes for at least thirty years. Until today, of course. Terror builds in me. My heart is thundering. I feel I could have a massive myocardial infarction and die here waiting to be killed.

I open my eyes. I wiggle a little. My sight starts to clear. Harry sits in front of me, looking at me. He knows I am awake. "Welcome back. I was hoping to avoid all this, you know. I thought I lost you back in Port Saint Lucie. I don't know how you managed to find me here."

I wasn't sure where you had gone after Port Saint Lucie, Harry. I always hoped I was wrong about you. Damn shame you have that black cloud following you. That and those horns growing out of your forehead make you look like Diablo himself."

"You always make me laugh, Matt. Guess that's why I kept you alive so long. Thought about killing you as far back as Assateague. But you are a good guy. Damn shame I have to burn you, but your being a good guy just makes it so sweet. It's difficult to explain why, but I do love it. You are a tough old bird, Matt. Promise me you won't just up and die when I get your first leg into the fire. I want you to hang on and beg a little at least."

He dumps my pack out on the ground, pulling it all the way inside out. Takes one of my cigars and lights it – sticks it in my mouth. "Enjoy yourself while you can Matt. This is not what's going to kill you." He lights one for himself, opens a can of corned beef hash and begins eating it cold. Then he picks up the cash that had fallen out. "Less than a hundred, Matt? I was sure you had more than that."

I puff my cigar very slowly. "Pissed it all away on wild women, Harry."

Harry finishes eating. "I need to be gone for awhile, Matt, watch out for bears."

As soon as he moves out of sight down the trail, I begin puffing harder on my cigar. I press the now hotly burning end against the duct tape closest to my mouth. Duct tape is strong and sticks to almost everything. If it is twisted, its strength is enough to lift a man. However, when it is flat, and the edge is cut a little, it can be easily ripped. I hope to burn enough of the edge to be able to rip it. Harry's return can be at any time, so I rush everything. I have succeeded it burning the edge of the tape, but I do not have the flexibility or strength to rip it the way it is taped now.

Harry did too good job taping me. My legs are cramping and my back hurts. If I don't do something fast, they will hurt a whole hell of a lot more.

I try to straighten my body, pulling hard with my back and legs. Nothing. I try to roll or wiggle my body to move it, thinking if I can get go the edge of the trail, I could roll down the mountain a ways. Nothing. I pull my hands and arms against my feet. I feel it give just a little. Ah, the Vaseline is working. It's gumming up the tape stick-um some.

I try to burn the tape a little farther with the cigar. It burns okay, but I still am not able to rip the tape. Spitting the cigar out of my mouth, I give up on the burn and rip plan. Let's concentrate on the tape slipping on my hands plan.

I open my fingers as wide as possible, then clench my fists. Pushing my fists together, I try to force my forearms out. Maybe I get a little stretch. I try to twist my forearms to the left and then back to the right. I know I can feel the tape slip a little. Now I pull as hard as I can against my feet. Can't tell if the tape is stretching or slipping just a little. Seems to be easier to open and close my hands though. I try to force my forearms out with my fists locked together, then begin twisting my forearms again. I am becoming desperate. I can see that the tape has slipped or stretched for several inches, giving me just a little freedom for my arms. I begin jerking my right, stronger arm, back as sharply as I can. I stop after five jerks. Tired, but I can see progress. Mortal fear gives me five more jerks. More room. I try to get my fingers to find one edge of the tape. I find the edge and begin working my fingers through the tape. I can see the tape move. I pull my fingers harder. I can actually see my fingers now. Pull, pull, twist, twist, lay back exhausted. It becomes a routine and a manta for me. Pull, pull, twist, twist, and on the third attempt, I slip my hand out through the opening.

Harry has taken the lanyard and my knife from my neck. He did not take the chain and my can opener. I bend into the tape this time, reach the chain with my hand, and flip it around until I find the can opener with my fingers. The short sharp edge is hard to work against the tape. I force myself to move slowly. I cannot lose the can opener. I finally manage to cut the tape nearest my hand. Then try to rip. Very little. Cut a little more, try to rip. Slow progress, but progress. Within five minutes, I have my hands free, then my arms, now I work on my legs, and soon I am tape free and standing.

I do not see Harry. I grab my staff, back pack, stuff everything back in the pack, and walk rapidly as I can down the trail away from the way Harry went. I wish I had my knife. Thirty minutes later, I begin walking on the grass at the edge of the trail, effectively removing any tracks. Thirty minutes after that, I go over the side of the mountain and down away from the trail.

I go about two hundred yards down the mountain. Find a nice crevice in between a huge tree and the side of the mountain. Work my way in tight. I am warm and well hidden. Perhaps, I will survive this.

At first light, taking stock: no knife, no gun, still have staff. I begin to pick up rocks. I need long distance damage or he will kill me. I use my can opener to cut off a two yard piece of fiberglass twine. Tie one end to a stout, four inch stick, then secure the other end to another piece of a stick. After I wrap the twine two or three times, I feel I have a serviceable garrote. Of course, I will try not to get close enough to use it.

I take off my tee shirt, put my jacket right back on. Rip the shirt in half, the long way. By tying the sleeves shut, and ripping the shirt down the side also, I have what I hope may be a serviceable sling. I put a rock into it, swing it around three times and let the rock fly. Damn, really flies hard compared with throwing. I hike back up to the trail, continuing to pick up stones about half the size of a baseball. When I reach the trail and level ground, I practice throwing with the sling. Within a half an hour, I find I can hit a man sized silhouette marked on a tree four times out of five throws at twenty feet. Time to destroy the Monster.

First, breakfast, coffee and stale bagel, then cigar. Mentally girding my loins, I hike down the trail towards where I last saw him. I continue to pick up stones as I walk, there are a lot of smooth ones, but I like the ones with edges on them. Stones go into jacket pockets, sling with one rock in it is in my right hand, I carry the staff in my left hand. I keeping looking for him, hoping he will be sleeping. When I finally see him, he is sitting, leaning against a tree, watching me.

"Sorry, Harry, but I gotta take you back. If you prefer, I will kill you here while you are in paradise. That way you can avoid all the jail time and the needle. I'm sure you know that soon you will have to be killed. I will do it as a friend and painlessly."

"How in the hell do you think you can kill me, Matt. I am stronger and faster than you. Your staff is useless against me. I would take it away from you and put it in the fire. I'm sorry, but I can't make a deal with you to kill you fast or painless. I just promise slow and painful. What makes you think you have a chance against me?"

"This," I say as I drop the staff from my hand and whirling the sling, let my first rock fly. It hits him mid-chest. By then my second rock is on its way and it hits him also. I hear a sharp 'konck' as it hits his head. As fast as I can pull the stones out of my pockets with my left hand, I sling them at him with my right hand. I am walking towards him and that helps my accuracy. I keep kicking my staff along as I move toward him. He is trying to stand but the rocks keep hitting him and he falls back. With three rocks left, I grab my staff, rush at him and swing that piece of hickory at him as hard as I can with both hands. It smashes against his left knee. He no longer tries to stand, he rolls to the right and off the side of the mountain, falling and rolling twenty feet before he regains his feet. He continues down the mountain, while I throw my last three rocks after him.

I hear him continue to crash down the mountain. He is at least two hundred yards below me. I cannot pursue him down the mountain. He is too fast, too nimble.

I salvage food and cigars from his pack, build a fire with the wood he has stacked up. I put his sleeping bag and pack into the fire. Black smoke curls into the trees. We are fifty miles from anywhere, the temperature during the days is in the sixties. Nights drop to down to low forties. No food, no dry clothes or sleeping bag, Harry will be dead in two days at the most from hypothermia.

I grab my back pack and begin hiking down the trail. I need to make sure he will be unable to get to me yet tonight. I hike at least five miles down the trail. I search the trees about me looking for the right wood. I find a young hazel tree about thirty feet high with several nice branches at least ten feet long. The branches are not as straight as I would like, but I have to use what's at hand. I cut both branches off the tree, split them down the middle. I manage to salvage one piece six feet long and one about four feet. I build a small fire and start to heat them slowly in the flames. I twist and turn them through the flames for about twenty minutes. I want to take out or dry up as much of the sap as possible. Laying the branches next to each other and with the ends of the shorter piece equal distance from both ends, I begin to tie them together with my nylon line. Three wraps around the wood and a square knot to secure it. Four knots in all. I cut a notch in the top and bottom of the long stake. Run my nylon line through the notches, pull the line until there is a bend in the stake, and tie the line to the front side of the bow. I try the strength of the bow. It pulls back easily at first, but then firms up and I take it to about twenty five pounds before I let up. I don't want to break it and I believe that it will put enough force behind an arrow to go through clothing and skin.

I begin searching for arrow wood. I find some willow shoots near a pond and cut all six that I find. They seem very straight and none have side shoots coming from them. I strip the bark, notch one side of the wood, carve the other end into a point, they harden both ends in the fire. I wrap the line around the notch in each arrow to prevent it from splitting up further. I would have liked to made proper arrowheads but I don't have enough time. Sharpened sticks will have to suffice. I make mac and cheese since I have a fire already built, then put the fire out, hike another several miles down the trail and settle in for the night. I put up the tent but sleep ten yards down the trail from it. Hopefully if Harry finds me, I will awaken when he looks in the tent.

I awaken at first light, cold and hungry. No hurry, I start a fire and make coffee. Eat one of the two bagels I have left and then pack up. I carry my sling, my bow and arrows, my knife on the lanyard around my neck, and I have put duct tape into my pocket. I hide the rest of my gear several hundred yards down from the trail.

I pick out a small target of bushes and at twenty five feet begin firing my arrows at the bushes. I get so I can hit it four out of five times. I know that will not necessarily be the same as firing at a person, but it is all I can do. I will not get more accurate today.

Now is the time for Harry hunting.

Back up the trail, bow with arrow notched, walking slowly, watching for everything. I feel there is a good chance that he will not have survived the night. I need to make sure. I am on high alert with my eyes searching every hiding place as I slowly walk. Listening carefully for the rustle of leaves. I am searching so hard and carefully that I almost walk into him.

He is lying at the base of a large oak. He is covered in leaves for warmth. I am unsure whether he is awake and I know I should shoot him where he lays but I am unable to. I just can't shoot him down like a mad dog.

"Harry, Harry, wake up."

"I'm awake, Matt. I'm just too cold to move."

"If you surrender and let me tape you up, I will take you back to my fire, then into town."

"Fuck you, Matt. What are you planning to do to prevent me from killing you and taking your clothes? I'm too close to you now for that rock sling." He is standing up as he says this. He is covered with mud and leaves. He looks like the yeti from hell.

At the first step he makes toward me, I let my first arrow go. It strikes him in the lower abdomen. Damn, not the shot I wanted to make. I quickly fire again, but the second bolt misses altogether. I am backing up away from him as I fire. By the time I notch the third arrow he is less than five feet from me and the arrow gets him in the throat. He reaches up and pulls it out. Grabs my bow and breaks it in half, then pulls the arrow from of his abdomen and he is on me. I have pulled my knife and grip it tightly, but the lanyard is still around my neck.

On his first rush, he knocks me backward giving me a little separation to clear the lanyard. I slash him across his chest as he grabs at me again. His blood spurts against me hot and thick. He throws me bodily to the ground and I smash my right shoulder hard against the rock-hard semi-frozen trail. I am dazed when he falls on me and begins trying to get his hands around my throat. I know if he is on me long enough, I will be too tired to fight back and keep rocking to get out from under him while at the same time, fight to keep his hands from grabbing for my throat. I push his hands back with my left hand. With my right hand, I pull the blade of the knife against his abdomen as I bring the knife back to my right side. He screams and rolls from me. I can see he is bleeding severely. The first slash against his chest, together with the arrow in the throat would have probably been sufficient to kill him. The abdominal cut drains his energies rapidly. I stand as fast as I can and ask him one more time to give up. "I can still save you, Harry." He grabs at me, and I plunge the knife into his forehead, killing him instantly. Unlike him, I cannot bear to watch any creature suffer.

I sit and look at him. I am in pain, exhausted and still have a ten mile walk back. I'm too fried to walk over and get a cigar. If he had not been drained by the cold and our fight from the previous day, he would have killed me. I am shaking where I sit. When the shakes subside and I gain a little strength, I stand to begin the walk back. Staff in hand, cigar in mouth, I trudge southward.

I stop at the Ranger Station to report Harry's death. First, by blind luck, I call Frank. I know he and Chuck will want to know.

Frank tells me, "Tell them someone attacked you and you had to defend yourself. Tell them where he is. Identify yourself, then shut up. Tell them you won't say more until you talk to a court appointed lawyer. The fact is you killed a man. He may have been a monster, but the courts don't consider that. You will have to make it self-defense or the legal system will have you guilty of murder. The more you keep your mouth shut at this point, the faster you will be free."

"Damn, good thing I called you, I hadn't really thought about that."

"I'm on my way, Matt. See you tomorrow or the next day. Love you Big Guy and thank you from my whole family."

Turned out much like Frank had said. Kept my reality to myself and ten days later, I was on my way back to Florida, a free man. Official account is that I was up in the park, practicing archery when I was attacked. My acts were self defense. I was fined $600 for injuring the trees. Strictly forbidden in the Smoky Mountains National Park, but since I was sincerely repentant, they gave me a minimum fine. The fines were easy though, turns out I qualified for $9000 worth of rewards for providing information that led to the apprehension of Harry.

CHAPTER TWENTY-THREE

TEDDIE

I am back staying with Top now for the last week. Been a little hassled by the police who seem to always have one more question and I have been interviewed by a local news reporter. As the lucky survivor of a vicious attack, I made the evening news for my ninety seconds of fame. I received a free dessert at the Cottage, when I had my last burger, and have been labeled Hero by most of the single women over sixty five here In Port Saint Lucie.

I am unsure how many casseroles a man can eat before he goes toes skyward, but the Ladies Delegation of Feeding Heroes seems determined to find out with me as the test subject. They are all very nice and Top Belton has developed a relationship with one pretty blonde lady. He is basking in the attention. One night he mentions to me that Polident actually tastes better than he thought it would.

"More information than I ever want to know, Top. We can let that discussion end right here." I am renting a home here now, from an absent owner. Thinking of buying it."

What I did purchase is a used pop-up trailer. I wanted one small enough to be towed behind the Jeep. Need more room now with my additional responsibly of Bogie and that soft bed speaks dulcet tones to these old bones. An inside toilet is extra luxury for the same price.

Since I still have some money left, I call Kill Devil Hill Rehab Center to see if I have a balance to settle. Nurse Teddie answers the phone. I am going to ask for the administrative office, when she says, "Hi Matt, I was wondering if you were going to call."

My heart skips ahead a little. "I love the sound of your voice, Teddie. You knew I had to call you. Hope all is going well for you."

"I was hoping you liked more than the sound of my voice, Matt. But, yes, things are going great here for me. That flatheaded slug I was married to ran off with a twenty two year old cocktail waitress. Leaving me here alone, all kinds of free and happy."

"Well beautiful lady, would you be interested in a visit from an older man who thinks you are one of the more enchanting creatures who ever walked the earth?"

"Damn Matt, I love the way you talk. And yes, I would like a visit from a crusty old dude who I think is cuter than a bugs behind. My vacation here starts in eight days. If you can make it by then, I will spend the whole two weeks with you."

"Yes, Yes, Yes, but maybe a counter proposal. If I send you a plane ticket, would you me in West Palm Beach, and then we head south to Key West for sunshine and genuine Sloppy Joes?"

Eight days later, I'm driving around West Palm Beach looking for the airport, collecting evil looks, horn honks, and being regularly saluted as I maneuver gracefully through traffic. Good thing I came to town three hours early. But I am on time to watch Lovely-Lovely walking up the hallway from the plane. She moves in a gentle halo of beauty and greets me with a kiss.

Four hours later, I back the camper into my brother-in laws driveway in Marathon, Florida. We get out, stretch and watch the ocean in the distance. Then we walk to the shore because everything in Florida is better with sand in your shoes and a sea shell in your hand. Going back, I level the camper. Unfortunately, Jeremy must have been unaware that I was coming and locked the back door, so I have to remove one panel of glass with my knife's handle, before I can get to his outlets, then I hook the water hose on and plug in the electric cord. I raise the top, and hooray, everything works. Oh Happiness. We are set up for the week.

Teddie goes into the bathroom first, when the water gets warm enough. I go in when she is finished and shower, brush my teeth and come back out, ready to face the world. Her hair is still radiant. I pat the bunk next to me for her to join me. She sits next to me and I gently kiss her neck. She has the sweet musky odor of a fresh honey dew melon just cut in two when the sweetness is rising on the air. "MMM, you look and smell wonderful."

She tells me about the nursing home on the days after I left. "Matt, you would have loved the chaos. It was pandemonium central for two days. You are legend at the home. A superman able to walk through walls," she smiles and chuckles as she tells me. When she turns to face me, I kiss her. Tell her, I missed her.

Then we decided to check the mattress and springs to see if the bed would be acceptable for sleep. We have no air-conditioning, temp is around 85, so we quickly manage to work up a sweat. In the afternoon light, bathed in perspiration, smiling, hopefully sated, she is a vision of beauty I will never forget.

I am not very knowledgeable about women. I have spent my life with one remarkable woman, now I have met another. I find that if I follow where they lead, I am well rewarded. Judging by the nips and cooing while we cuddle, Teddie is having a pretty good vacation. We dress for dinner. In the Keys, tees, shorts, and flip flops is considered formal wear. We head up to Long Pine Key for Coconut Shrimp and Pina Coladas. We sign the dollar bills and staple them to the wall as custom demands here at No Name Bar. Then we go for a long walk along the beach and back to Marathon and the camper. This is paradise.

She is up before me and has the coffee made. I find her standing outside watching the water. "I brought my fishing pole if you want to try."

"No, just like watching the water."

I light a cigar and agree with her.

"This is a great place, did you rent it?"

"No, it's my former brother-in-laws. He would have an angina attack if he knew I was here. He works during the week though so we have two more days before he comes down."

"Maybe we should leave if it would upset him."

"Oh this will more than upset him. When he gets the water and light bill he will probably have loose bowels for a week. He called my wife once because she had sent him a text message that cost fifteen cents. He forbade the sending of text messages. Do you know it costs a buck and a half every time you flush the toilet down here? Don't worry though. I have always enjoyed torturing him. He has plenty of money."

"Okay," she says, walks into the camper and flushes the toilet. "There goes ten text messages right down the drain." She is chuckling.

"That's the spirit."

"Let's plan tomorrow, Sweetheart, Key West, tourist crap, dancing parrots, jugglers and tee shirt shops, or shall we rent a boat and head out to a deserted Key where we can avoid everyone in the world who is unimportant?"

"Let's take the boat. We'll always have Key West."

"Ah, here's looking at you, Kid."

We walked down to The Brass Pot for a hand dipped ice cream cone and a few camping supplies. In the morning we drive up to Islamorada to rent a boat. We have to be back before Friday at noon if I am to move the camper before Pit Bull gets home.

I call Top to make sure all is okay with Bogie and to say we will be out of touch for a few days.

"Matt, I have bad news. Keith was robbed early yesterday when he opened. Whoever it was shot him three times. He's in a coma."

"Is there anything I can do to help?"

"Not really. I thought I should tell you. I will let you know if anything further develops."

It casts a pall over the morning for me. I don't tell Teddie. We ride out into the surf, north several blocks and then under the bridge heading for the leeward Keys. We search for an hour or so and then pick a Key with a nice beach and no people anywhere near us.

I pull the boat out, unload all our gear, then tip it over to keep the rain out. I tie it to a Brazilian pepper tree so it can't be carried away with a high tide. Ten minutes later, we have the camp set up. Teddie knows her way around a tent; ten more minutes we are in the ocean, going for that all over tanned look. She looks as good nude as she did in the tailored blues.

Perfect ocean temp around 75 degrees and air temp of 85 degrees. Florida. God created Florida for people in love.

We lunched on fried grouper sandwiches we had brought with us from Islamorada, then slip into the tent for an early afternoon nap.

At early twilight, I break out my fly rod and twenty minutes later, we're feasting on fresh snook. Perfect with the bottle of Chardonnay. We enjoy the evening talking of family and the past, how wonderful this evening is, and eventually the future. "I can move anywhere," I tell her, "but I am not trying to pressure you."

We sleep soundly in the gentle noises of the night and the ocean. We have one more full day before we return to civilization.

When I arise, I see the sun breaking the grip of the night. I walk out to the ocean's edge to light a cigar. A few minutes later, I wade in for an early swim to wash my face and hands. I am standing in waist deep water enjoying the sight of three dolphins barely rising above the water, when I feel the unique shisshh and vibration of a small caliber bullet going past my head.

"Run, Teddie, someone is shooting at us."

I dive under water, swim away from where I heard the round fired. I make it about fifteen feet before I feel a sharp pain in my back up near my right shoulder. My right arm refuses to work correctly and I am reduced to swimming with only my left hand. I hear at least six more shots fired at me. I work out in my mind this is a nine shot, 22 cal. Automatic pistol. Our attacker will need to change magazines or reload at this point. So I break for shore and begin walking as rapidly as I can away from our attacker. I feel a round hit my left leg, high up on the outside of the leg, only skin, but the blood begins to pour out.

I hear footsteps running up behind me. A woman's voice says, "Stop right there, Matt, or the next shot goes through you chest. I can't miss from here."

I stop, turn, a tallish woman has a gun pointed at me. I've never seen her before. "I'm Lorraine, I was Harry's wife. You ruined our lives. You promised him a job, sent him all the way here with a ton of hope, only to crush his dream. You destroyed our life. You heartless fuck, you deserve to die."

I can't think of a thing to say. I am weakened by the loss of blood, the pain in my back, and I can barely manage to say "aaaghhh," as I topple over on my face in the sand. I feel another bullet hit me before I sink into total darkness.

When I regain consciousness, I am on a bed, with sheets, white sheets, bed is uncomfortable as hell. Must be a hospital. To my left, I see Teddie, reading a book.

"I can see you, Beautiful."

"Matt, you're back. They weren't too sure you would live when we got you here. You had lost so much blood."

"You must have saved me. I know you're an Angel. Thank you for keeping me alive."

"Got that bitch with the camp hatchet. I whacked off her ear, she dropped the gun, and gave up. Turns out she shot some guy named Keith up in Port Saint Lucie. He told her we were in Key

West. She just got lucky and was going over the bridge at Islamorada and recognized you. Her husband had sent her a picture of you. Were you his friend or something?"

"Yes, I really liked her husband, Harry, until he turned out to be a serial killer, who was trying to kill me."

Right then the doctor comes in to check on me. Teddie has to leave. "I will be back tomorrow morning."

I drink down a couple glasses of water, feast on the sumptuous half-cooked hospital fare and try to fall asleep. It's a long restless night of pain and hospital bed torture. I flop and twist trying to find any position that is at least a little bit comfortable. Finally with the dawn, Lovely-Lovely comes in.

"Good morning, Matt," Teddie says, "How was the night?"

"Terribly lonely without you."

"I missed you too."

"Fill me in, what happened after I passed out?"

"I loaded you in the boat, took you back to Islamorada, luckily, I saw another boat on the way and they radioed in for an ambulance. They took you to the hospital, while I took the car back to get the camper from your brother-in-laws place. He was already down there when I pulled up and he helped me break down the camper. Jeremy is such a nice man. He is letting me stay at his place until you get on your feet. Did you know he has a Corvette?'

"Jeremy? You call that no-necked jerk, Jeremy?"

"He drove us up to Key Largo for pizza in his Corvette, two nights ago, and then last night, he gave me a ride on his Harley down to Key West, for a sloppy joe at Sloppy Joe's. I think you've misjudged your brother-in-law. He is a gentleman and very nice."

"Jeremy?" I ask incredulously. "You rode behind him on a motorcycle? Jeremy?"

"Matt, you know I am fond of you. I will always like you and want you to be my friend, but the truth is you scare the hell out of me. I need a quieter life than what you live. I really like Jeremy, but I won't pursue a relationship with him if it would hurt you."

"Honest to God now, Jeremy? You could actual kiss Jeremy?"

She walks out the door and doesn't look back.

While I am in shock thinking about anyone actually kissing that no-neck twerp, my doctor comes in.

"Mr. Castain, You have two bullets still in you, we plan on

taking them out next Tuesday. It's a simple operation and won't take long. What does concern me, is your PSI is very high, and we have found a tumor near where the previous cancer was removed. Given your history with Agent Orange, I don't think we can wait. I want to start intravenous chemo-therapy right now, and I recommend surgery on the tumor at the same time we remove the two bullets.

Now that's a hell-of-a-day, three bullet holes, a girl leaves me for my brother-in-law, and my cancer has come back. It's the Perfect Trifecta. Gotta be better news tomorrow.

ABOUT THE AUTHOR

David is a former U.S. Navy Corpsman who spent time attached to the Marine Corps. He earned a Bachelor's degree from Northwestern College, and a Master's degree at Western Illinois University. He currently lives in Port Saint Lucie, Florida with his wife and three dogs.

Made in the USA
Charleston, SC
06 September 2014